John Scott

Critical Essays on Some of the Poems of Several English Poets

Vol. 2

John Scott

Critical Essays on Some of the Poems of Several English Poets
Vol. 2

ISBN/EAN: 9783337406943

Printed in Europe, USA, Canada, Australia, Japan

Cover: Foto ©Andreas Hilbeck / pixelio.de

More available books at **www.hansebooks.com**

ESSAY VII.

On Gray's Church-Yard Elegy.

THE Elegy written in a Country
Church-Yard, from the nature of
its subject, and the merit of its executi-
ons, has obtained an uncommon share of
popularity. The principal respect in
which it has been supposed defective, is
a want of plan; an ingenious Writer has
observed, ' that it is thought by some to
' be no more than a confused heap of
' splendid ideas, thrown together with-
' out order, and without proportion.'*
That it is, however, not destitute of

---

* Mr. Knox's Essays, Moral and Literary, Vol. 1, p.
92, 1st. Edit.

plan,

plan, the following analyfis will fufficiently demonftrate : whether the arrangement might not have been in fome parts
improved, is another queftion.   The
Poet very graphically deferibes the procefs of a calm evening, in which he introduces himfelf wandering near a Country Church-Yard. From the fight of
the place, he takes occafion, by a few
natural and fimple, but important circumftances, to characterize the life of a
peafant ; and obferves, that it need not
be difdained by ambition or grandeur,
whofe moft diftinguifhed fuperiorities
muft all terminate in the grave.   He then
proceeds to intimate, that it was not
from any natural inequality of abilities,
but from want of acquired advantages,
as riches, knowledge, &c. that the
humble race, whofe place of interment
he was furveying, did not rank with the
moft celebrated of their cotemporaries.
The fame impediments, however, which
obftructed their courfe to greatnefs, he
                                     thinks

thinks alſo precluded their progreſs in vice, and, conſequently, that what was loſt in one reſpect, was gained in the other. From this reflection he not unnaturally proceeds to remark, on that univerſality of regard to the deceaſed, which produces, even for theſe humble villagers, a commemoration of their paſt exiſtence. Then turning his attention on himſelf, he indulges the idea of his being commemorated in the ſame manner, and introduces an epitaph which he ſuppoſes to be employed on the occaſion. The matter here, it muſt be allowed, is not extenſive nor uncommon; the poem muſt, therefore, depend much on the manner for its importance:

V. 1. The curfew tolls the knell of parting day;
    The lowing herd wind ſlowly o'er the lea;
    The plowman homeward plods his weary way,
    And leaves the world to darkneſs and to me.

    Now fades the glimmering landſcape on the
        ſight,
    And all the air a ſolemn ſtillneſs holds,
                                            Save

Save where the beetle wheels his droning flight
    And drowsy tinklings lull the distant folds;

Save that, from yonder ivy-mantled tow'r,
    The moping owl does to the moon complain
Of such, as wand'ring near her secret bow'r,
    Molest her ancient solitary reign.

Poetry can alone universally interest, when it "brings back the memory of the past," when it recalls the objects we have seen, and the emotions we have felt. Every man of observation, who has wandered in the fields in an autumnal evening, will acknowledge Gray's picture to be drawn from nature. The circumstances which denote the progression of time, are regularly introduced, and finely marked; as the departure of day;* the homeward return of the herd, and of the plowman; the gradual fading of the landscape; the subsequent silence, broken only by the hum of the beetle; the distant tinkling of the weather bell, and hooting of the owl;

* *Parting day* was undoubtedly intended for *fitting sun.*

and

and laftly, the rifing of the moon, by which the Church-Yard, the object of contemplation, becomes vifible.

Parallels between different fubjects are feldom natural or juft enough to be pleafing; they exift oftener in the fancy of the perfon comparing, than in any actual refemblance of the things compared. The e are inftances however, in which they have their advantages: the fuppofed tolling of the curfew, juft as the fun was leaving the horizon, is not wholly deftitute of analogy to the tolling of what is called the paffing bell for the deceafed. The mention of a knell, naturally recalls this idea, and fpreads a folemnity over the mind, which prepares it for the fentiments that follow.

A Periodical Writer * has objected to this line.

' The curfew tolls the knell of parting day.'

* THE BABLER, Vol. 1. No. 55.

The

The verb being ufed in the prefent, inftead of the preterite, *parting* inftead of
parted, produces (he thinks) a falfe metaphor, as the bell is never rung till
the perfon is dead. Among our ancef-
tors, however, the bell was rung while
the party was expiring, in order to obtain the prayers of the neighbourhood
on his behalf.*

There is an anachronifm, in intro-
ducing the curfew, a cuftom of a remote
period, in a modern poem, in which
the poet alfo introduces himfelf; but this
is a venial tranfgreffion of propriety, for
which the goodnefs of the poetry amply compenfates. This ftanza has, indeed, many beauties: there are, perhaps,
few inftances, wherein the fenfe is more
enforced by correfpondent found, than

---

* The very expreffion of *paffing* bell accords with this
idea. See BRAND's edition of BOURNE's Antiquita-
tes Vulgares, page 12.

in

in that of the ' *herd winding flowly o'er* ' *the lea*,' and that of the verb ' *plod*,' applied to the movement of the plow-man. The idea of folitude, always grand, and often pleafing, is ftrongly impreffed by the circumftance of the cattle, and the peafant relinquifhing the fields to the wandering poet.

The Beetle * was introduced in poe-try by Shakefpeare, but that circum-ftance is no proof of imitation in Gray; both poets undoubtedly transferred im-mediately from nature, an image fo very common. Shakefpeare has made the moft of his defcription; indeed, far too much, confidering the occafion :

* The name of beetle points out the *genus*, not the *fpecies* of infect. That here intended is the large black one, fo common in autumnal and mild wintry even-ings, as often to fly with confiderable force againft the faces of perfons walking abroad. This has been con-founded with a fummer beetle, viz. the common tree **cockchafer.**

To

———— ——To black Hecate's summons
The shard-born beetle with his drowsey hum,
Hath rung night's yawning peal.————

Macbeth, who had committed one murder in perfon, who intended to commit another by proxy, and was about to acquaint his wife with his intention, could not be very likely to talk of Hecate fummoning the beetle ' *With his drowfy* ' *hum to ring night's yawning peal;*' nor to recollect that fuch beetle had its place of nativity under a tile fhard.＊ The imagination muft be indeed fertile, which could produce this ill placed exuberance of imagery. The Poet, when compofing this paffage, muft have had in his mind all the remote ideas of Hecate, a heathen goddefs, of a beetle, of night, of a peal of bells, and of that action of the mufcles, commonly called a gape or yawn.

＊ Shakefpeare was remarkably fond of defcriptive minutenefs ; his beetle is *fhard-born*, his bat is *cloyfter'd*, with many other inftances of the fame kind, introduced with more or lef propriety.

Dr.

Dr. Hill, in his Natural History of Animals, has objected to the cause assigned by Gray, for the hollowing of the owl : the voice of that bird, he thinks, is not the voice of complaint, but rather of joy or exultation. Perhaps we are not sufficiently acquainted with the œconomy of nocturnal fowls, to decide positively what is the real occasion of their clamour. That it is produced by molestation, we have no reason to believe, because they are seldom molested, and often clamorous; that it is produced by pleasure, we have no certainty, nor are we more certain that it proceeds from hunger. Owls have been noticed to be more vociferous in the same places, in some years, and in some seasons of the year, than in others. During the breeding time, when the feathered race in general are most noisy, it is remarkable that this genus is uncommonly silent : two of these animals often seem to answer each other's voices; and a sin-

gle

gle one has fometimes feemed to chufe
a fituation, wherein its own voice might
be returned by an echo. The paffage
in queftion, however, is truly poetical;
and though it may affign a wrong caufe,
in a matter where we cannot affign a
right one, few perfons perhaps will wifh
it had been omitted.

V. 13. Beneath thofe rugged elms, that yew trees
   fhade,
  Where heaves the turf in many a mould'ring
   heap,
  Each in his narrow cell for ever laid,
   The rude forefathers of the hamlet fleep.

  The breezy call of incenfe-breathing morn,
   The fwallow twittering from the ftraw-
   built fhed,
  The cock's fhrill clarion, or the echoing horn,
   No more fhall roufe them from their lowly
   bed.

  For them no more the blazing hearth fhall
   burn,
   Or bufy houfewife ply her evening care;
  No children run to lifp their fire's return,
   Or climb his knees the envy'd kifs to fhare.
            Oit

Oft did the harveſt to their ſickle yield,
  Their furrow oft the ſtubborn glebe has *
    broke :
How jocund did they drive their team afield!
  How bow'd the woods beneath their ſturdy
    ſtroke!

The rural day is here moſt beautifully
depicted: the images are ſo obvious,
ſo natural in themſelves, and ſo naturally connected, that one is ſurprized
to find them now firſt placed in this
pleaſing point of combination. All the
circumſtances, except the morning
breeze, which is perhaps too poetically
made the voice of a proſopopoiea, ' *The*
' *breezy call, &c.*' are expreſſed without
diminution of dignity, in the ſimpleſt

---

* The other members of this ſtanza are ſimilar, with
regard to the notation of time; the verbs are all in the
ſimple preterite ; and if the meaſure of the verſe would
have allowed the omiſſion of the auxiliar *has*, this line
would have been of the ſame ſtructure, and been better.
If any auxiliar were admitted, I think it ſhould be the
preterpluperfect *had*, as ſpeaking of acts performed previous to a certain point of paſt time, viz. that of the
peaſant's deceaſe.

manner

manner imaginable; cottage life is delineated in the moſt pleaſing colours,
every thing amiable is introduced, every
thing diſguſting or ridiculous is ſup-
preſſed. There is, however, a love of
order in ſome minds, which would have
been better ſatisfied with a different
arrangement of theſe ſtanzas: the rural
morning, as in nature, might have been
immediately ſucceeded by the rural mid-
day, and the rural mid-day by the rural
evening. By this means alſo, the mind
would have repoſed on the pleaſing and
intereſting idea of the peaſant ſurround-
ed by his children.

> The breezy call of incenſe-breathing morn,
>   The ſwallow twittering from the ſtraw-built
>   ſhed,
> The cock's ſhrill clarion, or the echoing horn,
>   No more ſhall rouſe them from their lowly bed.
>
> Oft did the harveſt to their ſickle yield,
>   Their furrow oft the ſtubborn glebe has broke:

How

How jocund did they drive their team afield!
How bow'd the woods beneath their sturdy
stroke!

For them no more the blazing hearth shall burn,
Or busy housewife ply her evening care;
No children run to lisp their sire's return,
Or climb his knees the envy'd kiss to share.

The matter of transposition might, indeed, have been carried still farther; the business of the respective seasons might have been mentioned in regular progression:

Oft jocund did they drive their team afield,
Their furrow oft the stubborn glebe had broke:
How did the harvest to their sickle yield!
How bow'd the woods beneath their sturdy
stroke!

The poetry seems to suffer little or nothing from this alteration. One objection may perhaps arise, that by insisting on a multiplicity of diurnal acts, in driving the team afield, 'Oft jocund, 'Gc.' instead of a multiplicity of annual

N 3   operations,

operations, in gathering the harveft, '*Oft*
'*did, &c.*' we loofe the pleafing idea of
the fuppofed longævity of a ruftick.   It
may alfo be queftioned, whether the ex-
clamatory '*How,*' has not more pathos,
when applied to the mental hilarity of
the carter, than when applied to the corporeal energy or agility of the reaper.

V. 29. Let not ambition mock their ufeful toil,
     Their homely joys, and deftiny obfcure ;
  Nor grandeur hear, with a difdainful fmile,
    The fhort and fimple annals of the poor :

The pleonafm and periffology, have been
already difcriminated as bearing, one a
good fenfe, the other a bad one ; as
modes of fpeech, in both of which more
words are ufed than are abfolutely neceffary, but as modes of fpeech, effen-
tially different in their intention and
effect.*   The pleonafm is here beautifully
exemplified ; all, in fact, is faid in the firft
two lines of the ftanza, '*Let not, &c.*' that
is faid in the third and fourth ; but the ite-

* See page 43.

ration

ration is a climax that impreffes the idea with additional vigour. Few poetical images have been more ftrongly drawn, than this of ' *Grandeur fmiling difdain-* ' *fully at the annals of the poor.* '

> V. 33. The boaft of heraldry, the pomp of pow'r,
>   And all that Beauty, all that Wealth e'er
>   gave,
>   Awaits * alike the inevitable hour ;
>   The paths of glory lead but to the grave.

This ftanza is characterized by energy, and melody, in the higheft degree. Poetry attains her purpofe by various ways ; fometimes by fingle, and fometimes by combined efforts ; and where variety does not produce confufion, it often adds force. In a hiftory piece well executed, a number of perfons, all of diftinct character, but co-operating to one general end, will moftly enhance its

---

* It fhould have been *await*, the plural, for it includes a number of circumftances.

value.

value. We have here, firſt, a group of abſtract ideas, *'The boaſt of heraldry,* *'&c.'* ſo forcibly convey'd, that we almoſt imperſonate them in our own mind, as *'awaiting the approach of the* *'inevitable hour:'* the ſcene is then changed, and the ſame circumſtance repreſented in another manner; we ſee the *'paths of glory,'* however different or diſtant, all converging to, and concluding in, one central point, they *'lead but to* *'the Grave.'* It is obſervable, that the poet here properly confines himſelf to the gifts of fortune, *'The boaſt of heral-* *'dry, &c.* one inſtance only, that of beauty, excepted; thus artfully preparing us for his ſubſequent ſtanzas, *'Per-* *'haps in this neglected ſpot, &c.'* where he introduces the gifts of nature as equally common to the rich and the poor. If beauty, which, as a gift of nature, is at leaſt as frequent among the latter as among the former, had been totally omitted, the paſſage might have gained in point of regularity, though it would have loſt

loſt in point of pathos. That even Gray
could not unite all advantages, only
proves, that, in all human compoſitions,
there muſt be imperfection.

> V. 37. Nor you, ye proud, *impute to theſe the fault*;
>   If memory o'er their tomb no trophies raiſe,
>   Where thro' the long-drawn iſle and fretted
>   vault,
>   The pealing anthem ſwells the note of praiſe.
>
> Can ſtoried urn, or animated buſt,
>   Back to its manſion call the fleeting breath?
> Can Honour's voice provoke the ſilent duſt,
>   Or Flattery ſooth the dull cold ear of death?

The phraſe, ' *impute to theſe the fault*,'
does not ſeem very happily to expreſs
the poet's idea; which was obviouſly
this, that the great have no pretence to
deſpiſe the mean for the privation of thoſe
funeral honours, which can avail nothing
to the dead, of any rank whatever. The
ſecond ſtanza, ' *Can ſtoried urn, &c.*' aſks
queſtions, which ſurely need not have been
aſked, becauſe they can be anſwered only
                                       in

in the negative; they are, however, ask-
ed, with such dignity and grace, that we
must not only pardon, but admire them.

The Author of these Essays has known
so many instances of a coincidence totally casual, a resemblance of sentiment or expression, where there could
be no possibility of communication, that
he scarcely dares to say what he thinks
is, or is not, really a designed or acci-
dental imitation; or in other words,
where memory has, or has not, been
either consciously, or unconsciously con-
cerned. When Gray wrote these stanzas,
he possibly might have been reading
Tickell's beautiful Poem on the Death of
Addison; and the Westminster-Abbey
scene might consequently furnish some
of his *Disjecti Membra Poetæ*. This
however is by no means certain; a man
of Gray's disposition would undoubtedly
sometimes frequent our venerable Gothick
Cathedrals,

Cathedrals,* and might copy immediately from the originals, his ' *long drawn*
' *ifle*,' ' *fretted vault*,' ' *pealing anthem*,'
and ' *animated ftatue*.' Be this as it
may, it is at leaft worth obferving, how
nobly, yet, how varioufly, two great
mafters || have touched the fame fubject :

How filent did his old companions tread,
By midnight lamps, the manfions of the dead ;
Thro' breathing ftatues, then unheeded things,
Thro' rows of warriors, and thro' walks of
    kings !
What awe did the flow folemn knell infpire,
The pealing organ, and the paufing choir.—
                  TICKELL.

V. 4*. Perhaps in this neglected fpot is laid
    Some heart, once pregnant with celeftial fire ;
Hands, that the rod of empire might have
    fway'd,
Or wak'd to extafy the living lyre.

* We have GRAY's own authority for this. See MA-
    SON's edition of his Poems, &c. quarto, p. 26c.

|| TICKELL, however neglected his works may be, was
    really a genuine poet.

                              .But

But Knowledge to their eyes her ample page,
  Rich with the spoils of Time, did ne'er unroll;
Chill Penury repress'd their noble rage,
  And freeze the genial current of the soul.

Full many a gem of purest ray serene,
  The dark unfathom'd caves of ocean bear;
Full many a flower is born to blush unseen,
  And waste its sweetness on the desart air.

The English language probably cannot boast a finer specimen of poetry than these stanzas. The supposition of the powers possessed, of the circumstances which prevented their exertion, and the illustrative comparisons, are all communicated with a grandeur and energy that have seldom been equalled. The Poet calls from the graves before him, the hands that might have wielded the sceptre, or struck the lyre, and creates in our imaginations the allegorical beings, who repressed their progress to greatness; Knowledge with-holding the fight of her roll, and Penury casting on them a look, which

which might be metaphorically said to freeze or congeal their faculties.*

There is in Young's Night Thoughts, a profopopoiea of Midnight, waving a lift of mortality in the ftartled eye, or fight of Fancy :

> By the long lift of fwift mortality,
> From Adam downwards to this ev'ning's knell,
> Which Midnight waves in Fancy's ftartled eye.

Gray undoubtedly had read the lines, yet it is queftionable whether he thought of

* The defigner, and engraver, have more than once employed their refpective arts, in producing an embel-lifhment to this noble poem. The poet leaning over a tomb-ftone, given us by one, and the funeral poffeffion by another, are trite and obvious ideas. The ftanza in queftion would afford a fine picture : two of Gray's Fore-fathers of the hamlet, might be introduced repo-fing from their labour; dignity and grace might be given to their forms; the eye of one beaming celeftial fire, might caft a regretful look at Knowledge turning from him with her folded roll; the other might indig-nantly regard Penury, who at a diftance fhould, with a calm feverity of countenance, point out to him a plough, or fome other inftrument of that cultivation, which it was his lot to attend to.

them

them when he produced this not very
diffimilar image of Knowledge with her
ample page. The action of the perfon
is however properly varied, as the general fubject required; Midnight is ex-
pofing the contents of the roll, knowledge
is concealing them. There is in Pope's
Rape of the Lock, a paffage which poffibly fupplied our author with his fentiment; and there is in Young's Satires,
another to which he might be indebted
for his turn of expreffion:

> Like rofes that in deferts bloom and die.
>> Pope.
> Full many a flower is born to blufh unfeen.
>> Gray.
> And wafte their mufic on the favage race.
>> Young.
> And wafte their fweetnefs on the defert air.
>> Gray.

V. 57. Some village Hampden, that, with dauntlefs
    breaft,
    The little tyrant of his fields withftool;

Some

Some mute inglorious Milton here may reſt ;
  Some Cromwell guiltleſs of his country's
  blood.

The applauſe of liſtening ſenates to command,
  The threats of pain and ruin to deſpiſe,
To ſcatter plenty o'er a ſmiling land,
  And read their hiſtory in a nation's eyes,

Their lot forbade : nor circumſcrib'd alone
  Their growing virtues, but their crimes con-
  fin'd ;
Forbade to wade through ſlaughter to a throne,
  And ſhut the gates of mercy on mankind ;

The ſtruggling pangs of conſcious truth to hide,
  To quench the bluſhes of ingenuous ſhame,
Or heap the ſhrines of luxury and pride,
  With incenſe kindled at the Muſe's flame.

The doctrine which our poet had been
inculcating in general terms, and illuſ-
trating by remote ſimile, by the gem
and the flower, he here proceeds to il-
luſtrate, by ſuppoſed particular example ;
but ſome of the inſtances adduced in
exemplification, do not ſeem happily
diſpoſed. The mind is always beſt ſa-
                                    tisfied,

tisfied, when its finds the different parts of a paragraph, bearing either a cloſe analogy, or regular contraſt, of thought and expreſſion. The ' *Hands that might* ' *have borne the rod of empire,*' ſhould have been, as it were, realized in the mention of ſome monarch of ſuperior celebrity; as the ' *Hands that might have waked* ' *the living lyre,*' have their realization in the mention of Milton. Inſtead of this, we now meet with images of another character; Hampden a *patriot*, and Cromwell a *warrior*. The deſign, however, which is thus complex and confuſed, might have been rendered ſimple, if the radical ſtanza, ' *Perhaps in this* ' *neglected ſpot, &c.*' had ſtood totally unconnected with its ſucceſſors, which would have been the caſe, if the inſtance of Milton had been omitted. The *King* and the *Poet*, would then have been equally diſmiſſed, without perſonal repreſentation; and Hampden and Cromwell, the *Senator* and the *General*, would have

have become principals, to whom the two succeeding stanzas, ‘ *The applause* ‘ *of listening senates, &c,*’ would have borne a proper relation ; the senatorial attributes being naturally appended to the one, and the military criminalities to the other. Had this plan been pursued, the last stanza of the above quotation, ‘ *The struggling pangs, &c,*’ must have been suppressed ; and indeed it may be doubted, whether much loss would have been sustained by its suppression. Besides its too long suspending the close of the period, it contains sentiments perhaps not strictly just : it supposes an uniform innocence in humble life, which assuredly cannot be found there ; the villager will learn ‘ *to hide* ‘ *the pangs of struggling truth,*’ or in other words, to tell a lye with a good grace, as well as the politician or the trader ; nor will he often be behind hand with his superiors, in ‘ *quenching* ‘ *the blushes of shame,*’ or acquiring what

O   is

is commonly called a confummate ftock of impudence.

That which Gray has left imperfect, it may be thought (and perhaps juftly) pre-fumption to attempt to amend; to render the preceding obfervations more intelligible, is therefore all that is meant by the following alterations:

Perhaps in this neglected fpot is laid
    Some heart once pregnant with celeftial fire;
Hands that the rod of empire might have fway'd,
    Or wak'd to extafy the living lyre:

But knowledge to their eyes her ample page,
    Rich with the fpoils of Time, did ne'er unroll;
Chill Penury reprefs'd their daring rage,
    And froze the vigorous current of the foul:

Full many a gem of pureft ray ferene,
    The dark unfathom'd caves of ocean bear;
Full many a flower is born to blufh unfeen,
    And wafte its fweetnefs on the defart air.

Some village Hampden who with dauntlefs breaft,
    The little tyrant of his fields withftood;

                Some

Some bold aspiring Cromwell here may rest,
  Obscure, and guiltless of his country's blood:

The applause of listening senates to command,
  The threats of pain and ruin to despise,
To scatter plenty o'er a smiling land,
  And read their history in a nation's eyes,

Their lot forbad; nor circumscrib'd alone,
  Their growing virtues, but their crimes confin'd;
Forbad to wade through slaughter to a throne,
  And shut the gates of mercy on mankind.

There is another method by which this
passage might be rendered more regular.
The radical stanza, ' *Perhaps in this neg-*
' *lected spot, &c.*' specifies only simple
eminence, without adjunct of either good
or evil: the fourth stanza, ' *Some village*
' *Hampden,*' by its personal illustration,
rather prematurely introduces both, and
might therefore be expunged; the rest
would then consistently expatiate on those
qualities in a variety of their operations:

Perhaps in this neglected spot is laid
  Some heart, once pregnant with celestial fire;

Hand,

Hands that the rod of empire might have sway'd,
  Or wak'd to extafy the living lyre:

But knowledge to their eyes her ample page,
  Rich with the spoils of time, did ne'er unroll,
Chill penury repress'd their daring rage,
  And froze the vigorous current of the foul:

Full many a gem of pureſt ray ferene,
  The dark unfathom'd caves of ocean bear,
Full many a flower is born to blush unfeen,
  And waſte its fweetneſs on the defert air.

The applauſe of liſtening fenates to command,
  The threats of pain and ruin to defpife,
To fcatter plenty o'er a fmiling land,
  And read their hiſtory in a nation's eyes,

Their lot forbad; nor circumfcrib'd alone,
  Their growing virtues, but their crimes confin'd,
Forbad to wade through flaughter to a throne,
  And fhut the gates of mercy on mankind.

But who, even for the fake of regularity, could admit fuch an alteration?
who could bear to lofe the recollection
of fuch national and intereſting examples, the recollection of a Hampden, a
Milton, and a Cromwell?

The

The Periodical Writer before-mention-
ed, feems to have perceived that this
part of the Elegy was in fome manner
defective; but not underftanding it fully,
he has accufed it of faults with which it
is not chargeable: 'The author,' fays
he, ' in the very moment that he intend-
' ed to lafh Cromwell with the greateft
' feverity, introduces him in the fame
' company with Hampden and Milton,
' the objects of his higheft admiration;
' and laments, in the fame introductory
' paffage, that

> Chill penury reprefs'd his noble rage,
> And froze the genial current of his foul.

' It is odd,' continues he, ' that a *noble*
' rage fhould ever be a *guilty* one.'

This is mifreprefentation; the Critic has
made the nonfenfe which he cenfures.
The paffage, which he juftly terms *introductory*, occurs before any mention is

O 3 made

made of Hampden, Milton, or Cromwell: it refers only to the Peasants, who are suppofed to have poffeffed powers equal to the powers of thofe celebrated characters, but without opportunity of expanding them into action. Hampden, Milton, and Cromwell are, it is true, introduced in company, not as common objects of praife, but as common poffeffors of the *nible rage* which had been mentioned, a neutral expreffion, by which I underftand no moral quality, either good or evil, but merely that *vivida vis animi*, which capacitates for great actions, whether virtuous or vicious in their own nature. With the fame erroneous idea, he proceeds to the context, ' *The applaufe of* ' *liftening fenates, &c.*' ' Here,' fays he, ' Cromwell is allowed his fhare of virtue, as well as Hampden and Milton; ' and they, in the pronoun plural *their,* ' are dragged in for their fhare of vices, ' as well as the celebrated ufurper.'

But

But the pronoun plural *their* relates neither to Hampden, nor Milton, nor Cromwell, but to two claffes of rufticks, who, if circumſtances had favoured the exertion of their abilities when living, might either have benefited or injured their fellow creatures: ſuch of them as had virtue in their reſtricted ſphere, would only have been more conſpicuouſly good; ſuch of them as had vice, would only have been preeminently wicked.*

This paſſage has been ſufficiently conſidered, with regard to its ſenſe; ſome attention ſeems now due to its expreſſion:

> To ſcatter plenty o'er a ſmiling land,
> And read their hiſtory in a nation's eyes.

* This Writer's objections may ſeem unneceſſarily attended to; but as his Eſſay is the only profeſſed Criticiſm on GRAY's Elegy, it ſeemed to require ſome notice.

Poetical

Poetical boldnefs, carried to its utmoft claffical limit, is inftanced in thefe lines. Some of the images are fo uncertainly marked, that we fcarcely know whether they were intended for natural objects or allegorical perfonages. ' *Plenty*,' indeed, which is very often perfonifed, cannot poffibly be fo here; for the circumftance of being ' *fcattered*,' precludes the idea of a perfon, and fixes the meaning to the actual produce of cultivation. The ' *land*,' from the application of the epi-thet ' *fmiling*,' may be regarded as a perfonification, but perhaps nothing more was really defigned, than the mere extent of the country; which when re-plenifhed with flowers, fruits, and corn, is frequently faid to *fmile*. The next line, ' *And read their hiftory, &c.*' ranks in a ftill more doubtful predicament. We are at a lofs to determine, whether we are to underftand by the word ' *na-* ' *tion*,' the croud of individuals, the real people at large, in *propria perfona*, or the fame fubject confidered in the aggregate,

as

as comprehended in one sublime imaginary existence. The first idea undoubtedly occurred first to the poet, and might produce the second, which was probably what he meant to convey to the reader. The metaphor in this line, ' *And read their history, &c.*' though considerably removed from simplicity, does not seem to violate propriety: the emotions of the mind are, it is well known, visible to a certain degree in the countenance; and by a long established mode of speech, which exchanges a general for a specifick term, instead of saying we *perceive*, we say we *read* them. The Author then had not passed the bounds of custom, in supposing of patriots or heroes, that they read admiration or reverence in the eyes of a nation; but he goes further, and, by a metonymy of effect for cause, supposes that they read there, the history of those actions, for which they are admired or revered. To illustrate his sentiment by example, were easy; the late

Duke

Duke of Cumberland, after the battle of Culloden, and the late Earl of Chatham at the close of the war, 1763, must have been beheld with such obvious gratitude, that they might be said to ' *read* ' *their hiſtory in a nation's eyes.*'

It is worthy obſervation, that the circumſtance which Gray has thus dignified, and repreſented as glorious and enviable, Pope has degraded, and endeavoured to render an object of contempt :

> One ſelf-approving hour whole years outweighs,
> Of ſtudied flarers, and of loud huzzas.

Gray's expreſſion, it may be ſaid, involves the whole publick ; the moſt reſpectable part of it the opulent and intelligent, as well as the vulgar ; Pope alludes only to the latter. But that Pope's ſentiments of popularity, even with the higher ranks of mankind, were

not

not very favourable, his Essay on Man,
in another place, sufficiently demonstrates :

> And more true joy Marcellus exil'd feels,
> Than Cæsar with a senate *at his heels.*

The people of all classes are indeed so variable in their opinions, so
prompt extravagantly to applaud, and
capriciously to censure, that a popular
man may fairly consider his reputation
as a cloud before the wind, perpetually
varying its form, now increasing, now
diminishing, and at length dispersed
in air.

> Forbad to wade through slaughter to a throne,
> And shut the gates of mercy on mankind.

The image of wading through blood, has
no great claim to novelty; but it is introduced with dignity and propriety. There
is sufficient analogy between him who
should literally wade through blood to a
throne,

throne confidered as a local eminence; and him by whofe command blood is fhed, in order for his obtainment of political fuperiority. The image in the next line is equally grand and appofite; a tyrant's inflexibility, could not, perhaps, have been defcribed with more force, than by faying he ' *fhut the gates of mercy on man-* ' *kind.*'

> Or heap the fhrine of Luxury and Pride,'
> With incenfe kindled at the Mufe's flame.

The metaphors here are common, but they are not unpleafingly applied. The ' *Mufe's flame kindles incenfe*;' that is, Poetical genius offers flattery at the fhrine of Luxury and Pride. *Shrine*, by a bold *licentia poetica*, is here fubftituted for *altar*. Dr. Johnfon defines a fhrine, ' *a cafe in which fomething facred is repo-* ' *fited*;' a fhrine confequently cannot properly be faid to be heaped at all, and much lefs properly with incenfe; an

altar

altar is the place appropriated to that material.*   The Muse's flame here mentioned, has not, however, very often kindled the incense which has heaped the al-
tars of Luxury and Pride; Poetry has had
little concern with the volumes of rhym-
ing praise that have issued from the press;
Dryden's adulatory pieces, some of them
at least, excepted.   Mason, in one of his
Elegies, has finely characterized that Author, and with a metaphor less common and more beautiful than Gray's,
has represented him as crowning the
subjects of his applause with jewels:

If Pope through friendship fail'd, indignant view,
    Yet pity Dryden; hark, where'er he sings,
How adulation drops her courtly dew
    On titled rhymers and inglorious kings.

See from the depths of his exhaustless mine,
    His glittering stores the tuneful spendthrift
    threw,

* With our minor Poets and Poetesses, the words fane,
shrine, altar, &c. are perpetually in use, and are as
perpetually misapplied and confounded by them.

As

As fear or intereſt bids, behold they ſhrine,
   Now deck a CROMWELL's, now a CHARLES's
    brows.
           ELEGY to a YOUNG NOBLEMAN.

V. 73. Far from the madding crowd's ignoble ſtrife,
   Their ſober wiſhes never learn'd to ſtray;
   Along the cool ſequeſter'd vale of life,
   They kept the noiſeleſs tenor of their way.

To a reader, who does not think while
he reads, there is an ambiguity in this
paſſage, which may lead to a ſenſe contrary to the real one. The author ſuppoſes, that his peaſants were ſituated remote from the ' *crowd's ignoble ſtrife,*'
and that their wiſhes never ſtrayed towards it. The pronoun perſonal, ' *They,*'
with which *far* the adverb of ſituation
ſhould have connected, being not expreſſed, but only underſtood, that adverb
may be erroneouſly combined with
wiſhes, and of courſe it may be ab-
ſurdly thought, that the ruſtick's de-
ſires, inſtead of never extending to the
                    tumult

tumult of publick life, had never extended beyond it. There is here alſo a
trifling incongruity of ſentiment; that
ardour of action which had before been
pointed out as *glorious*, is here inadvertently termed *ignoble*. The two laſt
lines of the ſtanza, ' *Along the cool,*
' *&c.*' are a kind of obſcure or indirect alluſion, or ſimile :—the perſons
in queſtion, *held their quiet even courſe
through the world, like a ſilent ſtream
through a cool and ſolitary valley.*
The idea of the peaſants being content-
ed with their ſituation, is poetically
pleaſing, but not juſt. There is perhaps
no claſs of men, on the whole, more
diſſatisfied with its condition, or whoſe
wiſhes are more perpetually ſtraying to
the condition of others, than this. The
gentleman, the clergyman, the opulent
farmer, and the tradeſman, are the con-
ſtant objects of the ruſtick's envy ; ſuch,
alas, is unhappy human nature !

V. 77.

V. 77. Yet ev'n thefe bones from infult to protect,
  Some frail memorial ftill erected nigh,
 With uncouth rhyme and fhapelefs fculpture
   deck'd,
  Implores the paffing tribute of a figh.

  Their name, their years, fpelt by th' unletter'd
   Mufe,
   The place of fame and elegy fupply;
  And many a holy text around fhe ftrews,
   That teach the ruftick moralift to die.

  For who, to dumb Forgetfulnefs a prey,
   This pleafing anxious being e'er refign'd;
  Left the warm precincts of the chearful day,
   Nor caft one longing ling'ring look behind?

  On fome fond breaft the parting foul relies,
   Some pious drops the clofing eye requires;
  Ev'n from the tomb the voice of nature cries,
   Ev'n in our afhes live their wonted fires.

The great merit of a poet is not, like
Cowley, Donne, and Denham, to fay
what no man but himfelf has thought,
but what every man but himfelf has
thought, but no man exprefled, or at
leaft exprefled fo well. Dr. Johnfon
        has,

has, with great juſtice, allowed the originality of the above ſtanzas; ' I have ' never,' ſays he, ' ſeen the notions in ' any other place; yet he that reads ' them here, perſuades himſelf that he ' has always felt them.'

The general ſight of a Cemetery, naturally affects the mind with an unmixed and painful melancholy; it produces gloomy reflections on the end of all things, regret for others, or apprehenſion for ourſelves; but the Unlettered Muſe, with her little narratives, often introduces other ideas; her language is ſometimes ſo abſurd, that in a leſs ſerious ſituation, it would excite riſibility; and her tale is ſometimes ſo pathetically circumſtantial, that it awakens all our tenderneſs.

Nothing can be more noble, nothing can be more beautiful, and yet nothing

P   more

more fimple and intelligible, than the firft three ftanzas of the above quotation, ' *Yet ev'n thefe bones, &c.*' and they are fo correct, that they have not an epithet but what adds force to the fenfe, nor a rhyme that obfcures or weakens it. The fourth ftanza, ' *On fome fond breaft, &c.*' at leaft the latter part of it, is not quite perfpicuous. When the Poet tells us that the parting foul, or expiring perfon, relies on fome fond breaft, fome affectionate relative, we underftand that it fo relies for commemoration; but what is intended by thefe lines feems rather doubtful:

Ev'n from the tomb the voice of nature cries,
Ev'n in our afhes live their wonted fires.

The ancients, it is well known, were anxious, to an extreme, for funeral honours: they even fuppofed that the fpirits of the deceafed could not reft, till the rites of fepulture were performed.*

* See this opinion finely exemplified in the ftory of Patroclus, Iliad, Book 23.

Perhaps

Perhaps our author, with the licence of a poet, here adopts this claſſical opinion. If this was not his idea, it is difficult to ſay what could be. '*The voice of Na-'ture*,'* in the boſoms of the living, might indeed, be ſaid to cry, or call for ſuch tokens of regard to the dead, as we imagine may be acceptable to them; but this ſenſe it is evident was not intended here, for if it was, the voice of nature could not be ſaid to cry '*from the tomb*.'

Antiquity held another doctrine, which alſo ſeems here to be alluded to, viz. that, after death, the ſoul retained its uſual paſſions and affections, and conſequently might look to the objects of theſe paſſions or affections for proofs of their tender remembrance. Mr. Maſon, who allows the paſſage to be obſcure, thinks this to be the meaning. 'He meant to 'ſay,' ſays he (ſpeaking of the poet) 'that 'we wiſh to be remembered by our

* A poetical phraſe for the dictates of natural affection.

P 2   'friends

' friends after our death, in the same
' manner, as, when alive, we wished to
' be remembered by them in our ab-
' sence.'

The above-mentioned ingenious Writer
has given two variations of the last
line, one as it stood in the first edition,
and one of his own proposing:

Awake, and faithful to her wonted fires.—
Awake, and faithful to her first desires.—

These alterations, however, seem not to
render the sense much clearer; the last
is indeed the simplest, because it drops
the metaphor.

Ev'n in our ashes live their wonted fires.

This line, which is an avowed imitation of Petrarch,* inculcates the idea
of a posthumous connexion of the intellectual and corporeal part of man; the

* Son. 169.

spirit

spirit is supposed to be some how combined with, or concealed under, the dust, like fire in embers. Dr. Young, in a verse, which, from his aukward introduction of the verb *slumbers*, has puzzled many a juvenile reader, seems to reprobate this idea:

> Why then their loss deplore, that are not lost?
> Why wanders wretched thought their tombs
> around,
> In infidel distress? Are angels there?
> Slumbers,* rais'd up in dust, æthereal fire?

V. 93. For thee, who mindful of th' unhonour'd dead,
Dost in these lines their artless tale relate;
If chance, by lonely contemplation led,
Some kindred spirit may inquire thy fate,

* This verb, by being used in the singular at the opening of the line, so resembles the noun plural, that, without attention to the note of interrogation, we might mistake and make the line nonsense. The use of the auxiliary *can*, would destroy the ambiguity, render the culinary term *rais'd*, unnecessary, and improve the melody of the line:

> Can fires æthereal slumber in the dust?

Haply,

Haply, some hoary-headed swain may say;
   ‘ Oft have we seen him at the peep of dawn,
 ‘ Brushing with hasty steps the dews away,
    ‘ To meet the sun upon the upland lawn.’

   ‘ There at the foot of yonder nodding beech,
     ‘ That wreathes its old fantastic roots so
      ‘ high,
  ‘ His listless length at noontide would he
     ‘ stretch,
    ‘ And pore upon the brook that babbles by.’

  ‘ Hard by yon wood, now smiling as in scorn,
    ‘ Muttering his wayward fancies he would
     ‘ rove;
  ‘ Now drooping, woeful, wan, like one for-
    ‘ lorn,
    ‘ Or craz’d with care, or cross’d in hope-
     ‘ less love.’

Gray, in one of his letters, perhaps too
precipitately, asserts, that description
(by which he doubtless meant description
of rural scenery) never ought to make
the subject of poetry; but he admits it
to be its most graceful ornament; and
both at the beginning, and towards the
close of this beautiful Elegy, has most
                 advantage-

advantageously availed himself of it.
Thofe Criticks, who have denied this
Poem the merit of a general plan, have
miftaken general plan for proper difpo-
fition of particular parts; the former,
as has been fhewn, it really peffeffes; in
the latter, I have already noticed a defi-
ciency. Here is another inftance, wherein a fimple tranfpofition would, at leaft
in my opinion, produce a very confiderable improvement. The Poet's morning
perambulation is narrated in this ftanza,
' *Haply, fome hoary-headed fwain, &c.*'
his noontide repofe is defcribed in the
next, and he is introduced in the laft,
though without fpecification of time, re-
fuming his walk again. Had the firft
and third ftanzas been brought together, the unity of action would have been
preferved uninterrupted; the morning
wanderings would have been connected
in one point of view, and the noon-day
reft have naturally followed them; for
inftance:

P 4 ' Haply,

' Haply, some hoary-headed swain may say;
    ' Oft have we seen him at the peep of dawn,
' Brushing with hasty steps the dews away,
    ' To meet the sun upon the upland lawn.'

' Hard by yon wood, now smiling as in scorn,
    ' Muttering his wayward fancies he would
        ' rove ;
' Now drooping, woeful, wan, like one forlorn,
    ' Or craz'd with care, or cross'd in hopeless
        ' love.'

' There at the foot of yonder nodding beech,
    ' That wreathes its old fantastic roots so high,
' His listless length at noontide would he stretch,
    ' And pore upon the brook that babbles by.'

These stanzas have great merit. The rapid transitions of thought in the mind of a poet, as indicated in external action, are painted in the most lively manner. The rural imagery has an air of novelty ; and the beach, with its old fantastick roots, hanging over the rill, is a complete picture. Mr. Mason observes of the language in this part, that it has a dorick delicacy. It has, indeed, what I should rather term a happy rusticity, un-

degraded

degraded by meanness: from such a character as is represented speaking, ' *a hoary-*
' *headed swain,*' one should reasonably ex-
pect such phrases as these, ' *Hard by yon*
' *wood, &c.*' ' *wayward fancies,*' ' *woeful*
' *wan,*' ' *one forlorn,*' ' *craz'd with care,*'
' *crofs'd with love, &c.*'

The same Gentleman has favoured us
with a stanza, which, in Gray's M.S.
immediately succeeded the above, and
which he rather wonders the Poet should
have suppressed, as it would have completed the account of his whole day,
whereas evening is now omitted:

> Him have we seen the green-wood side along,
>   While o'er the heath we hied our labour done;
> Oft as the woodlark pip'd her farewell song,
>   With wistful eyes pursue the setting sun.

The stanza, considered in itself, is not a
bad one; but Gray was right in sup-
pressing it, and I think it is easy to con-
jecture some of the reasons for its suppression.

preffion. The Poet's evening had been
defcribed before, at the opening of the
Poem; to have defcribed it again,
would have been fuperfluous, and an
inftance of that difgufting redundance,
which is fure to create confufion, and
which we always meet with in the
works of common writers. Diverfity of
fituation alfo is wanting; we had the
wood before, ' *Hard by yon wood*;' and
now we have it again, ' *The green-wood*
' *fide along, &c.*' There is, indeed, a
kind of contraft, or antithefis, between
the idea in one of the former ftanzas, of
the poet going out to meet the fun at its
rife, and the idea in this ftanza, of his
viewing it with wiflful or regretful eyes
when fetting; but this contraft, as it is
here managed, does not pleafe; the
mention of the fun by name twice, at
leaft in its prefent pofition, has too much
famenefs to be agreeable.

V. 109. One morn I mifs'd him on the 'ccuftom'd hill,
    Along the *heath*, and near his favourite tree;
                    Another

Another came; nor yet beside the rill,
Nor up the *lawn*, nor at the *wood* was he.

The foregoing stanzas, p. 230, ' *Haply,*
' *some hoary-headed swain, &c.*' contain
subjects which ought to have been regularly and distinctly recapitulated or contrasted in this conclusion. This however is not the case. The ' *upland lawn,*'
in the first stanza, and the ' *nodding*
' *beech*;' and the ' *brook,*' in the second,
are well enough opposed by the ' *custom'd*
' *hill,*' the ' *favourite tree,*' and the ' *rill,*'
in the first, second, and third lines here;
but the ' *lawn,*' to which ' *custom'd hill,*'
had already corresponded, is now redun-
dantly introduced again by its own appellation, and the ' *wood,*' which would have
been more consistently expressed by some
synonymous term, is likewise simply
mentioned by name. The ' *heath,*' is a
new and superfluous image. These it
may be said are trifles, scarcely worth
notice; but if such trifles were more
regarded, composition would make
nearer

nearer approaches to perfection. The following arrangement is submitted to the Reader merely as explanatory of my own ideas:

Haply, some hoary-headed swain may say;
  Oft have we seen him at the peep of dawn,
Brushing with hasty steps the dews away,
  To meet the sun upon the *upland lawn* :

Hard by yon *wood*, now smiling as in scorn,
  Mutt'ring his wayward fancies he would rove;
Now drooping, woeful, wan, like one forlorn,
  Or craz'd with care, or cross'd in hopeless love.

There, at the foot of *yonder nodding beech*,
  That wreathes its old fantastic roots so high;
His listless length at noontide would he stretch,
  And pore upon the *brook* that babbles by.

One morn I miss'd him on the *custom'd hill*,
  Along the *copse*, and near his *favourite tree*;
There came another, and another still;
  Nor at the *grave*, nor by the *rill*, was he.

The first half of the last stanza, has here a proper relation to all the preceding objects, except the *brook*; the 'upland lawn,' is contrasted by the '*hill*,' the '*wood*' by the '*copse*,' and the '*beach*' by the '*tree*:'
                                                    the

the second half introduces only the *wood*, under the appellation of *grove*; and for the first time, contrasts the *brook* by the denomination of *rill*. These variations, however, do not obtain all the regularity that might be wished for; but perhaps they have as much as could be obtained in the same compass. The third line, '*There came another, &c.*' some may think rather injured in strength and sweetness by the alteration.

V. 113. The next, with dirges due in sad array,
   Slow through the church-way path we saw
    him borne.
   Approach, and read, (for thou canst read)
    the lay,
   Grav'd on the stone beneath that aged thorn.

I once heard it observed by a very ingenious Gentleman, that in Spenser's Fairy Queen, and Fairfax's Tasso, may be found almost every modern melody, every pleasing disposition of words in use with the poets of the present day.
          This

This is certain, that in different authors, we often meet with the fame turns of expreſſion, which neverthelefs is no proof of imitation. The fentiment in this line, ‘ *Approach and read*’ (*for thou canſt read*) ‘ *the lay*,’ undoubtedly produced the words, without adverſion to the language of any preceding writer ; for to convey it in words more natural, is not poſſible : yet fome may imagine they have found its prototype in this of Dr. Young ;

And fleal (for you can fteal) celeſtial fire.

In fome of the early editions of the Elegy, after the ſtanza laſt quoted, the following was inferted :

There, fcatter’d oft the earlieſt of the year,
    By hands unfeen are *flowers of violets* found ;
The red breaſt loves to build and warble there,
    And little footſteps lightly print the ground.

Mr. Mafon, who thinks thefe lines very fine, neverthelefs thinks they were very
                                                properly

properly omitted, becaufe they made the parenthefis too long. They had, indeed, this bad effect; but there were, I think, other caufes for their rejection. The preceding ftanza, ' *The next* ' *with dirges, &c.*' and this, are totally different in character; that is ferious, this is trifling; that deals in real fact, this in puerile fancies: the addition was like that of a Chinefe roof to a Tufcan column. Thefe corrections of Gray's, together with many hints in his letters, have convinced me that his poetical powers, however great, were not fuperior to his critical fkill.

E P I T A P H.

Here refts his head upon the lap of earth,*
    A youth, to fortune, and to fame, unknown.
Fair Science frown'd not on his humble birth,
    And Melancholy mark'd him for her own.

Large was his bounty, and his foul fincere;
    Heav'n did a recompence as largely fend:

——— * How glad would lay me down,
As in my mother's lap.———
                        Paradife Loft, B. 10, p. 777.
                                                    He

He gave to misery, all he had, a tear;
　He gain'd from heav'n ('twas all he wish'd) a
　　friend.

No farther seek his merits to disclose,
　Or draw his frailties from their dread abode;
(There they alike in trembling hope repose)
　The bosom of his father, and his God.

Respecting this Epitaph, of the two first stanzas, little need be said; they are both correct; the first is elegant and simple, the second is not totally clear of affectation. The turn of wit, by which the poet's '*large bounty*' is discovered to be only a '*tear*,' and his '*recompence*' is found in '*friendship*,' is certainly unexpected, and perhaps too refined for the occasion. To the third stanza, the Minor Critick, before quoted, strongly objects. " If it has any meaning," says he, " it can mean nothing but this," " that " it is improper to examine the merits " or frailties of the person deceased, " since they are both alike reposed in
　　　　　　　　　　　　　　　" one

" one dread abode, the bosom of his
" father and his God." ' This is the
' first time,' continues he, ' I ever heard
' of a human creature making the bo-
' som of his deity a repository for his
' errors; and in the present case, I
' think the fault more inexcusable, be-
' cause the violence offered to reason and
' religion, has no way assisted the poe-
' try, this being perhaps as lame a pas-
' sage as any in the whole piece.'* This
severe censure is unmerited: universal
custom has established and authorized
the substitution, however violent .or
awkward, of *bosom* for *mind*; and
taking the word in that sense, the
passage is defensible, and intends no
more than this: " That the merits and
" defects of the party in question
" were known to his maker, which was
" sufficient." What violence is here
committed, either against reason or re-

* The BAELER, vol. 1. p. 241.

ligion,

ligion, it is not eafy to difcover. That
the lines convey no new information;
that they tell nothing but what every
man muft know, is indeed evident;
and that, confidered as poetry, they
have no very confpicuous excellence, is
certain.

The attention that has been paid to
this Elegy, however particular, will not,
it is hoped, be thought tedious or fuperfluous. The Poem itfelf is, perhaps, the
firft of the kind in any language: its
fubject, like the fubject of Milton's Epic,
is univerfally interefting; the allegorical
imagery is fublime, and the natural defcription graphical; the fentiment is
moftly fimple and pathetick, and the verfe
has a melody which has not often been
attained, and cannot be furpaffed.

Gray's Poems are not numerous; but
all of them, at leaft his ferious Pieces,*
have

* GRAY's talents were indeed confined to the ferious.
In the few Pieces he has given us of a light caft, both in
profe

have great merit; and whoever writes but as correctly as he has written, will not find himself able to write much: happily, however, for some authors, it is often the bulk, rather than the correctness of productions, that now confers popularity.

The Church-Yard Elegy, as Mr. Mason justly observes, was Gray's most popular production. His two Greater Odes have been accused of obscurity; but one can be obscure to those only, who have not read Pindar; and the other, only to those, who are unacquainted with the history of our own nation. But it is needless to enlarge on these, as ample justice has been very lately done them by my friend Mr. Potter, the justly celebrated translator of Æschylus and Euripides.*

There

---

prose and verse, in his Long Story, his Drowned Cat, and in some of his Letters, the humour is at best faint, and often puerile.

* I cannot here forbear transcribing a passage from GRAY's works, which Mr. MASON thinks was proba-

bly

There is mention made, in Mr. Mason's Edition, of an intention of setting the second of these Odes to musick, in the manner of an Oratorio; and some of Gray's ideas on the subject are there preserved. My knowledge of musick is but superficial; but I lament that this design did not take place, as I think it would have afforded an opportunity of conveying whatever sound can convey, of the sublime and pathetick. Dryden's

bly written, on occasion of the common preference given to his Elegy. To the doctrine it contains, I yield my most hearty assent. " The Gout de Comparaison, as " BRUYERE stiles it, is the only taste of ordinary " minds. They do not know the specific excellency, " either of an author or a composition: for instance, " they do not know that TIBULLUS spoke the language " of nature and love; that HORACE saw the vanities " and follies of mankind with the most penetrating " eye, and touched them to the quick; that VIRGIL " ennobled even the most common images, by the graces " of a glowing, melodious, and well adapted expres- " sion: but they do know that VIRGIL was a better " Poet than HORACE, and that HORACE's Epistles do " not run so well as the Elegies of TIBULLUS."

famous

famous paſſage, ' *See the Furies ariſe,*'
&c. might perhaps be rivalled for ani-
mation of imagery by the concluſion of
the ſecond ſtrophe,

> She wolf of France, with unrelenting fangs,
> That tear'ſt the bowels of thy mangled mate,
> From thee be born, who o'er thy country hangs,
> The ſcourge of heav'n. What terrors round him
>   wait !
> Amazement in his van, with flight combin'd,
> And ſorrow's faded form and ſolitude behind.

The above Author's ' *Fallen! Fallen!*
' *Fallen!*' might alſo poſſibly have its
parallel for mournful melody in the
opening of the ſecond antiſtrophe,

> Mighty victor, mighty Lord,
> Low on his funereal couch he lies !
> No pitying heart, no eye afford
> A tear to grace his obſequies.
> Is the ſable warrior fled ?
> Thy ſon is gone. He reſts among the dead !—

There might likewiſe be a fine tran-
ſition from this pathetick to the exult-
ant,

ant, in

> Fair laughs the morn, and foft the zephir blows, &c.

But hints of this kind are unneceffary; Oratorios, and almoft every thing elfe that is ferious, are now out of fafhion.

I mentioned the Paper in the Babbler as the only profeffed Criticifm on Gray's Elegy. I have fince feen a pamphlet intitled, " A Criticifm on the Elegy " written in a Country Church-Yard," in which that Poem feems to have been examined on principles very diffimilar to mine.

ESSAY

E S S A Y VIII.

On GOLDSMITH'S DESERTED VILLAGE.

THE Temple of Fame, lately erected under the title of The Works
of the Englifh Poets, affords a ftriking
inftance of caprice in the matter of admiffion to literary honours. Had Criticifm, rational impartial criticifm, kept
the gate of this temple, feveral names
which now appear within its walls,
would certainly never have appeared
there. But to drop the allegory, and
change an imaginary edifice for a real

Q 4   book,

book, it is difficult to guess the reason why that book admitted some authors, while others of similar character were rejected.

Poet is an appellation frequently used, without the annexion of its precise idea; which seems to be that of a person who combines picturesque imagery, and interesting sentiment, and conveys them in melodious and regularly measured language. This is a definition, which will exclude the writer of Romances, and Prose Dramas, however sublime or pathetick, on the one hand; and the meer maker of Verses, however humorous or witty, on the other: were indeed the claim of either to be allowed, it must be that of the former; inasmuch as poetry must be nearer allied to the dignified and elegant, than to the mean and indelicate.

The

The title of Poet has been often bestow-
ed on those who little deserved it. The
name of English Classicks was surely ill-
merited, either by the Wits of Charles's
days, that "mob of gentlemen who wrote
with ease," or by the heroes of the Dun-
ciad; their compositions were mostly
trifling, and frequently immoral, and
consequently unworthy of preservation.
But in an Edition of poetry, where some
of these are to be found, we rather
wonder at not finding the others; where
Rochester and Roscommon, Sprat, Halli-
fax, Stepney, and Duke, were received,
why Carew, and Sedley, and Hopkins,
were refused, one is puzzled to guess;
and when Pomfret and Yalden are pre-
ferred to Eusden and Duck, it is not
easy to account for the preference.
The managers of this celebrated Edition,
as their work approached the present
period, seem to have been more fasti-
dious in their choice, and have omitted Writers who would have done their
collection

collection no difcredit.* When the Publication was undertaken, Armftrong and Langhorne, poets of fuperior rank, were living; their works, confequently, could not be prop rly inferted; but Goldfmith was dead, and his certainly had a juft claim to admiffion.

Goldfmith's Deferted Village, the work now under confideration, is a performance of diftinguifhed merit. The general idea it inculcates is this; that commerce, by an enormous introduction of wealth, has augmented the number of the rich, who by exhaufting the provifion of the poor, reduce them to the neceffity of emigration. This principle

---

* Among fuch may be reckoned AARON HILL, who although in general a bombaftick writer, produced fome Pieces of merit, particularly the CAVEAT, an allegorical fatire on Pope: ROBERT DODSLEY, author of Cleone, a Tragedy, and a Didactick Poem on Agriculture, intitled Publick Virtue: GRAINGER, tranflator of Tibullus, and author of another Didactick, called the Sugar Cane: CAWTHORN, author of Abelard to Eloifa, &c. &c.

is

is exemplified in the description of Auburn, a Country Village, once populous and flourishing, afterwards deserted and in ruins.

Modern poetry has, in general, one common defect, viz. the want of proper arrangement. There are many poems, whose component parts resemble a number of fine paintings, which have some connexion with each other, but are not placed in any regular series. The Deserted Village would have pleased me better, if all the circumstances relative to Auburn the inhabited, had been grouped in one picture; and all those relative to Auburn the deserted, in another. The Author's plan is more desultory; he gives us, alternately, contrasted sketches of the supposed place in its two different situations:

The Poem opens with an apostrophe to its subject:

V. 1.

V. 1. Sweet Auburn, *loveliest* village of the plain,
    Where health and plenty chear'd the *labouring*
        swain ;
    Where smiling spring its earliest visit paid,
    And parting summer's lingering blooms delay'd.
    Dear *lovely bowers* of innocence and *ease,*
    Seats of my youth, when ev'ry *sport* could please ;
    How often have I loiter'd on thy green,
    Where humble happiness endear'd each scene.
    How often have I paus'd on every charm,
    The shelter'd cot, the cultivated farm ;
    The never-failing brook, the busy mill,
    The decent church, that topt the neighb'ring
        hill.
    The hawthorn bush, with seats *beneath the shade,*
    For talking age, and whispering lovers made !
    How often have I blest the coming day,
    When *toil remitting* lent its turn to play,
    And all the village train from *labour free,*
    Led up their sports beneath the spreading tree ;
    While many a pastime circled in the shade,
    The young contending as the old survey'd ;
    And many a gambol frolick'd o'er the ground,
    And flights of art, and feats of strength went
        round.
    And still as each *repeated pleasure* tir'd,
    Succeeding sports the mirthful band *inspir'd ;*
    The dancing pair, that simply sought renown
    By holding out to tire each other down ;

                                    The

The swain mistrustless of his smutted face,
While secret laughter titter'd round the place ;
The bashful virgin's side-long looks of love,
The matron's glance, that would those looks
    reprove ;
These were thy charms *sweet* village ; *sports* like
    these
With *sweet succession taught e'en toil to please* ;
These round thy *bowers* thy chearful influence
    shed,
These were thy charms—But all these charms
    are fled.

This passage is one of that kind, with which the imagination may be pleased, but which will not fully satisfy the judgment. The four lines, ' *Dear lovely bowers,*' &c. might perhaps have been spared. The village diversions are insisted on with too much prolixity. They are described first with a puerile generality, redundance, and confusion : they are *sports*, and *pastimes*, and *gambols*, and *flights of art*, and *feats of strength* ; and they are represented sometimes as passive, the ' sports are *led up* ;' sometimes as active,

                the

the ' paſtimes *circle*,' and the gambols
' *frolick*,' and the ' flights and feats *go*
' *round*.' But we are perhaps fully re-
compenſed for this, by the claſſical and
beautiful particularity and conciſeneſs
of the context, ' *the dancing pair*,' ' *the*
' *ſwain miſtruſtleſs of his ſmutted face*,'
the ' *baſhful virgin's looks, &c.*' The
paragraph in general has much inaccuracy, eſpecially a diſguſting identity
of diction; the word ' *bowers*,' occurs
twice, the word ' *ſweet*,' thrice, and
' *charms*,' and ' *ſport*,' ſingular or plural, four times. We have alſo ' *toil*
' *remitting*,' and ' *toil taught to pleaſe*,'
' *ſucceeding ſports*,' and ' *ſports with*
' *ſweet ſucceſſion*.'

> *V*. 35. *Sweet ſmiling* village, *lovelieſt of the lawn*,
> Thy *ſports* are fled, and all thy *charms* with-
> drawn;
> Amidſt thy *bow'rs* the *tyrant's hand* is ſeen,
> And *deſolation ſaddens all thy green*:
> One only maſter graſps the whole domain,
> And half a tillage ſtints thy *ſmiling* plain;

No

No more thy glaffy brook reflects the day,
But chok'd with fedges, works its weedy way.
Along the glades a folitary gueft,
The hollow-founding bittern guards its neft;
Amidft thy defert walks the lapwing flies,
And tires their echoes with repeated cries.
Sunk are thy *bowers* in fhapelefs ruin all,
And the long grafs o'er tops the mould'ring
     wall,
And trembling, fhrinking, from the fpoiler's
     hand,
Far, far away thy children leave the land.

The paffage already examined, and this,
have both the fame character of verbofity. There is a repetition which indicates intention, and maintains regularity; and there is a repetition which
difcovers either carelefinefs, or poverty
of language. Auburn had before, l. 1.
been termed '*fweet*,' and '*the lovelieft*
'*village of the plain*;' it is now termed
'*fweet*,' and '*fmiling*,' and '*the love-*
'*lieft of the lawn*.' We had been told,
l. 34. that '*all its charms were fled*;'
and we are now told that '*its fports are*
                                    '*fled*,

' *fled, and its charms withdrawn.*' The
' *tyrant's band*,' feems mentioned rather
too abruptly; and ' *defolation faddening*
' *the green*,' is common place phrafeo-
logy. The eight lines, ' *No more the*
' *glaffy brook, &c.*' are natural and beautiful; but the next two, ' *And trembling*,
' *fhrinking, &c.*' are ill-placed, for they
prematurely introduce the fubject of
emigration.

> V. 51. *Ill* fares the land, to haftening *ills* a prey,
> Where wealth accumulates, and men decay;
> Princes and lords may flourifh, or may fade;
> A breath can make them, as a breath has
>   made;
> But a bold peafantry, their country's pride,
> When once deftroy'd can never be fupply'd.
>
> A time there was, e're England's griefs
>   began,
> When every rood of ground maintain'd its man;
> For him light labour fpread her wholefome ftore,
> Juft gave what life requir'd but gave no more:
> His beft companions innocence and health,
> And his beft riches ignorance of wealth.

The

The firſt of theſe paragraphs, ‘ *Ill fares*
‘ *the land, &c.*’ with all its merit, which
is great, for the ſentiment is noble, and
the expreſſion little inferior, ſeems
rather out of place; after the affair of de-
population had been more fully deſcribed, it might have appeared to advantage
as a concluding reflection. The ſecond
aſſerts what has been repeatedly denied,
that ‘ *there was a time in England, when*
‘ *every rood of ground maintained its man.*’
If however ſuch a time ever was, it
could not be ſo recent as when the De-
ſerted Village was flouriſhing, a circumſtance ſuppoſed to exiſt within the remembrance of the poet; conſequently
the idea had no buſineſs in the poem.

V. 63.   But times are alter'd; trade's unfeeling train,
    Uſurp the land, and diſpoſſeſs the ſwain;
    Along the lawn, where ſcatter'd hamlets roſe,
    Unweildly wealth, and cumb'rous pomp re-
      poſe;
    And every want to opulence allied,
    And every pang that folly pays to pride.
          R.   Thoſe

Those *gentle hours* that plenty bade to *bloom*,
Those calm desires that ask'd but little room,
Those healthful *sports* that grac'd the peaceful
   scene,
Liv'd in each *look*, and *brighten'd* all the
   green ;
These far-departing, seek a kinder shore,
And rural mirth and manners are no more.

This passage is a mere superfluity. The
first six lines, ' *But times are alter'd*,'
might have been reserved for introduction in some other part of the piece.
The next, ' *These gentle hours, &c.*'
should have been totally suppressed :
' *gentle hours* that *are bade to bloom*,' and
' *healthful sports* that *live* in *looks*, and
' *brighten a green*;' is certainly not vin-
dicable language. The ' *hours*,' and the
' *sports*' also, are said to ' *seek a kinder*
' *shore*,' which ' *kinder shore*,' is inconsistently described in the sequel of the
poem, as fraught with every inconve-
nience and every danger. The mention
of the ' *sports*,' and of the emigration,
                        ' *These*

' *These far-departing, &c.*' is here again unnecessarily repeated.

V. 74. *Sweet* Auburn! parent of the blissful hour,
　　　Thy glades forlorn confess the *tyrant's* power.
　　　Here as I take my solitary rounds,
　　　Amidst thy tangling walks, and ruin'd grounds,
　　　And, many a year elaps'd, return to view,
　　　Where once the cottage stood the hawthorn
　　　　　grew,
　　　Here, as with doubtful, pensive steps I range,
　　　Trace every scene, and wonder at the change,*
　　　Remembrance wakes with all her busy train,
　　　Swells at my breast, and turns the past to pain.

The adjective ' *sweet*,' is frequently, and very properly, in use as a substitute for agreeable or pleasant, but it displeases in this work by perpetual repetition. The obscure and indefinite idea of a ' *Tyrant*,' recurs also unnecessarily here again. There is pathos in the lines, ' *And many*

---

　* An unquam patriæ longo post tempore fines,
　　Pauperis et tuguri congestum cespite culmen,
　　Post aliquot mea regna videns mirabor aristas?
　　　　　　　　　　　　　　　　　V I R G.

　　　　　' *a year,*

' *a year, &c.*' but they are as evidently
misplaced as some of their predecessors:
we wish to hear more of the Village in
its prosperity, before we hear so much
of its desol   n.

Subsequent to the above, we have an
expatiation on the Author's fallacious
hope of concluding his days at his favourite Auburn, and a paragraph in
praise of retirement; both well written,
but rather episodical.

V. 115. *Sweet* was the sound, when oft at ev'ning's
         close,
     Up yonder hill the village murmur rose;
     There as I past with careless steps, and slow,
     The mingled notes came soften'd from below;
     The swain responsive as the milk-maid sung,
     The *sober* herd that low'd to meet their young;
     The noisy geese that gabbled o'er the pool,
     The playful children just *let loose* from school;
     The watch dog's voice, that bay'd the whisp-
         'ring wind,
     And the loud laugh, that spoke the vacant
         mind;
                                        These

These all in soft confusion *sought the shade,* *
And fill'd each pause the nightingale had made.
But now the sounds of population fail,
No chearful murmurs fluctuate in the gale,
No busy steps the grass-grown footway tread,
But all the *bloomy flush of life is fled.*
All but yon widow'd solitary thing,
That feebly bends beside the plashy spring;
She wretched matron, forc'd, in age, for bread,
To strip the brook with mantling cresses spread,
To pick her wintry faggot from the thorn,
To seek her nightly shade, and weep till morn;
She only left of all the harmless train,
The sad historian of the *pensive* plain.

This is indeed a passage of uncommon merit. The circumstances it describes are obvious in nature, but new in poetry; and they are described with great force and elegance. Milton, in a simile,

---

* The village murmur, l. 116, is said ' to have risen
' up the hill;' it is now said to have ' sought the shade.'
This seems at first sight an inconsistency, but perhaps the
poet may be vindicated by supposing that the hill, like
many other hills, was shaded with trees. Perhaps if
a rhyme had not been wanted, we should not have met
with the word ' shade,' on this occasion.

R 3   which

which he thought capable of illustrating the idea of an Eden, among other objects of delight has introduced

Each rural fight, each rural found.—

The Epic Poet, however, only mentions found in the general, but our Author descends to particulars, and those particulars are most happily selected; they bear one uniform consistent character, viz. that of a sober or serene chearfulness. The locality given by the intimation, that they were heard '*from be-* '*low*,' has a fine effect. In Paradise Lost, b. v. l. 547. we have a beautiful instance of the same kind:

Cherubic fongs, by night from neigh'b'ring hills, Aerial mufic fend. '——

The *Matron gathering water-crefses,* is a fine picture; but there is unnatu-

* The fituation is here reverfed, the fongs proceed from above.

ral

ral exaggeration in representing her as
' *weeping*,' every night, ' *till morning* ;'
sudden calamity occasions violent emotions, but habitual hardship will not
produce inceffant forrow ; time recon-
ciles us to the moft difagreeable fitua-
tions. Our Author's language in this
place, is also very defective in correctnefs. After mentioning the general
privation of the ' *bloomy flufh of life*,'
the exceptionary, ' *all but*,' includes, as
part of that ' *bloomy flufh*,' an ' *aged de-*
' *crepid matron* ;' that is to fay, in plain
profe, ' *the bloomy flufh of life is all fled*
' *but one old woman*.'

The Poet now recurs again to the paft.
When Auburn is defcribed as flourifh-
ing, its Clergyman as a principal inha-
bitant, is very properly introduced.
This fuppofed Village Paftor, is characterized in a manner which feems almoft unexceptionable, both for fentiment and expreffion. His contentment,

hospitality, and piety, are pointed out
with sufficient particularity, yet without confusion or redundance. Where in-
discriminate approbation can be hazard-
ed, quotation is the less necessary; but
probably few readers will think the following extracts tedious.

> Near yonder copse, where once the garden
> smil'd,
> And still where many a garden flower grows wild;
> There, where a few torn shrubs the place disclose,
> The village preacher's modest mansion rose.

This is a fine natural stroke.—We see
the ' *copse*,' the ' *torn shrubs*,' and the
' *scatter'd flowers*.' The last remaining
vestige of what was once a garden, is
always the ' *garden flower that grows
' wild*.'

> A man he was, to all the country dear,
> And passing rich with forty pounds a year;
> Remote from towns he ran his godly race,
> Nor e'er had chang'd, nor wish'd to change
> his place;

Unskilful

Unskilful he to fawn, or seek for power,
By doctrines fashion'd to the varying hour;
Far other aims his heart had learn'd to prize,
More bent to raise the wretched, than to rise;
His house was known to all the vagrant train,
He chid their wand'rings, but reliev'd their
    pain.—
—Pleas'd with his guests, the good man learn'd
    to glow,
And quite forgot their vices in their woe;
Careless their merits or their faults to scan,
His pity gave e'er charity began.

The benevolent mind cannot but yield
its hearty assent to this beautiful oblique
reprehension of that avarice which makes
the crimes and errors of the poor, a pretence to justify the indulgence of its
own parsimony.

—At church with meek and unaffected grace,
    His looks adorn'd the venerable place;
    Truth from his lips prevail'd with double sway,
    And fools who came to scoff, remain'd to pray.
    The service past, around the pious man,
    With steady zeal the honest rusticks ran;
    Ev'n children follow'd with endearing wile,
    And pluck'd his gown to share the good man's
    smile:

His

His ready fmile a parent's warmth exprefs'd,
Their welfare pleas'd him, and their cares
 diſtreſs'd ;
To them his heart, his love, his grief, were
 given,
But all his ferious thoughts had reſt in heaven.
As fome tall cliff that lifts its awful form,
Swells from the vale, and midway leaves the
 ſtorm ;
Though round its breaſt the rolling clouds
 are fpread,
Eternal funſhine fettles on its head.

Poetry attains its full purpofe, when
it fets its fubjects ſtrongly and diſtinctly
in our view. This is the cafe here : we
behold the good old man attended by his
venerating pariſhioners, and with a kind
of dignified complacence, even permit-
ing the familiarities of their children.
The concluding fimile has been much
admired, and fo far as immaterial objects
can be illuſtrated by material, it is
indeed a happy illuſtration.

As every parifh has its Clergyman,
almoſt every parifh has its School-maſter.
 This

This secondary character is here described with great force and precision. The Muse, in part of her description, has descended to convey village ideas, in village language, but has contrived to give just so much dignity to the familiar, as prevents it from disgusting. The point is indeed so nice, that to say the lines in italicks are not prosaick or mean, is perhaps to say all that can be said truly. We are reconciled to them only, because we know that they are the effect of choice, not of incapacity:

> Beside yon straggling fence that skirts the way,
> With blossom'd furze unprofitably gay,
> There in his noisy mansion, skill'd to rule,
> The village-master taught his little school;
> A man severe he was, and stern to view,
> I knew him well, and every truant knew.
> Well had the boding tremblers learn'd to trace,
> The day's disasters in his morning face;
> Full well they laugh'd with counterfeited glee,
> At all his jokes, for many a joke had he;
> Full well the busy whisper circling round,
> Convey'd the dismal tidings when he frown'd;
>   Yet

Yet he was kind, or if severe in aught,
The love he bore to learning was in fault :
The village all declar'd how much he *knew* ;
'Twas certain he could write and cypher too ;
Lands he could measure, terms and tides pre-
    sage,
And e'en the story ran that he could gage :
In arguing too the parson own'd his skill,
For e'en though vanquish'd, he could argue
    still ;
While words of learned length and thund'ring
    sound,
Amaz'd the gazing rusticks rang'd around,
And still they gaz'd, and still the wonder grew,
That one small head could carry all he knew.

The description of the Village Ale-
house, contains domestick minutiæ, of a
kind, which must necessarily have pleased in the original, but which the hand
of a master alone, could have made to
please in the copy. That learned and
judicious Critick, Dr. Warton, in his
Essay on the Writings and Genius of
Pope, justly observes, that ' The use,
' the force, and the excellence of lan-
' guage, consists in raising clear, com-
                                    ' plete,

' plete, and circumstantial images, and
' in turning readers into spectators.'
This theory he exemplifies, by quoting
two passages from his author, in which,
he says, that ' every epithet paints its
' object, and paints it distinctly.' The
same may be said with equal justice of
the following :

Near yonder thorn, that lifts its head on high,
Where once the sign-post caught the passing
  eye ;
Low lies that house, where nut-brown draughts
  inspir'd,
Where grey-beard mirth, and smiling toil re-
  tir'd ;
Where village statesmen talk'd with looks
  profound,
And news much older than their ale went round.
Imagination fondly stoops to trace,
The parlour splendors of that festive place ;
The white-wash'd wall, the nicely sanded floor,
The varnish'd clock that click'd behind the
  door ;
The *chest* contriv'd a double debt to pay,
A bed by night, a *chest* of drawers by *day* ;
The pictures plac'd for ornament and use,
The twelve good rules, the royal game of goose ;
                                         The

The hearth, except when winter chill'd the
    day,
With afpen boughs, and flowers and fennel gay,
While broken tea cups wifely kept for fhow,
Rang'd o'er the chimney, glitter'd in a row.

This fine poetical inventory of the furni-
ture, is fully equalled by the character
of the guefts, and the detail of their
amufements. The negative mode of
expreffion, ' *Thither no more, &c.*' by
fixing the mind on the paft, adds a kind
of pleafing regretful pathos :

Vain tranfitory fplendors ! could not all
Reprieve the tottering manfion from its fall !
Obfcure it finks, nor fhall it more impart
An hour's importance to the poor man's heart ;
Thither no more the peafant fhall repair,
To fweet oblivion of his daily care ;
No more the farmer's news, the barber's tale,
No more the woodman's ballad fhall prevail ;
No more the fmith his dufty brow fhall clear,
Relax his pond'rous ftrength, and lean to hear ;
The hoft himfelf no longer fhall be found,
Careful to fee the mantling blifs go round ;
Nor the coy maid, half willing to be preft,
Shall kifs the cup to pafs it to the reft.

This

This is not poetical fiction, but historical truth. We have here no imaginary Arcadia, but the real country; no poetical swains, but the men who actually drive the plough, or wield the scythe, the sickle, the hammer, or the hedging bill. But though nothing is invented, something is suppressed. The rustick's hour of relaxation is too rarely so innocent; it is too often contaminated with extravagance, anger, and profanity: describing vice and folly, however, will not prevent their existing; and it is agreeable to forget for a moment, the reality of their existence.

The foregoing description not unnaturally introduces the following reflections:

> Yes! let the rich deride, the proud disdain,
> These simple blessings of the lowly train;
> To me more dear, congenial to my heart,
> One native charm, than all the gloss of art;
>
>   *Spontaneous*

Spontaneous joys, where nature has its play,
The soul adopts, and owns their first-born sway:
Lightly they frolick o'er the vacant mind,
Unenvy'd, unmolested, unconfin'd.
But the long pomp, the midnight masquerade,
With all the *freaks* of wanton wealth *array'd*,
In these, e're triflers half their wish obtain,
The toiling pleasure sickens into pain;
And, ev'n while Fashions brightest arts decoy,
The heart distrusting asks, if this be joy?

The sentiment here is better than the expression. The Poet is probably right in his supposition, that the pleasures of the rich are less genuine and lively than those of the poor; but his language is far from being simple or perspicuous. That intention and parade raise expectations which will be mostly disappointed; that the joys which are unanticipated, and unconstrained, or independent of the will of others, are the best; were undoubtedly the axioms intended to be conveyed in these lines, ' *Spontaneous joys, &c.*' By ' *spontaneous* ' *joys,*' we must understand, joys which

without

without previous care or provision seem to offer themselves to our acceptance: to say that the soul readily accepts such, might be proper; but to say that the soul ' *adopts*' them, and at the same time ' *owns their sway*;' ' and to say that the ' *sway*,' is a ' *first-born sway*;' is to use thoughts and words not clear of confusion: but when these joys which the ' *soul adopts*,' and whose ' *first-born sway* ' *it owns*,' are said to ' *frolick over the* ' *mind lightly, unenvied, unmolested, and* ' *unconfined*;' we have surely a chaos, both of ideas and phraseology.* The lines have also an ambiguity: we know not whether it is meant, that ' *the soul adopts spontaneous joys*,' in which

* To discover fully the nonsense of this passage, it is necessary to recur to the sense of the words metaphorically used. The *joys*, from the verb *adopt*, must be supposed to be children, something inferior, or dependent; from the substantive *sway*, they must be supposed to be kings, something superior, or governing; and from the verb *frolick*, one conceives an idea of a set of mischievous young rakes, or of a harlequin. The *soul adopts the joys*, and they *rule it*, and *frolick over it*.

S   ' *nature*

' *nature has her play* ;' or that ' *where*
' *nature has her play, the soul adopts*
' *spontaneous joys* :' be the sense what it
may, it is superfluous, and superfluities
always create obscurity. There is a most
extraordinary confusion of ideas, in the
' *long pomp*' and ' *midnight masquerade*
' *array'd*' in the ' *freaks of wanton*
' *wealth* :' how pomp and a masquerade
could be ' *array'd* ' at all, is not easy
to conceive ; but certainly they could
not be ' *array'd* ' with ' *freaks*.'

The Poet now proceeds to the causes
which produced the desertion of his
village :

Ye friends to truth, ye statesmen, who survey
The rich man's joys increase, the poor's decay ;
Tis yours to judge, how wide the limits stand
Between a splendid and a happy land.
Proud swells the tide with loads of freighted ore,
And shouting folly hails them from her shore ;
Hoards, ev'n beyond the miser's wish, abound,
And rich men flock from all the world around.
Yet count our gains : this wealth is but a name,
That leaves our useful product still the same.
Not so the less : the man of wealth and pride,
Takes up a space that many poor supplied ;

Space

Space for his lake, his park's extended bounds,
Space for his horses, equipage, and hounds·
The robe that wraps his limbs in silken sloth,
Has robb'd the neighb'ring fields of half their growth.
His seat, where solitary sports are seen,
Indignant spurns the cottage from the green;
Around the world each needful product flies,
For all the luxuries the world supplies.
While thus the land adorn'd for pleasure all,
In barren splendor feebly waits its fall.

Goldsmith undoubtedly was serious in the foregoing apostrophe, ' *Ye friends* ' *to truth, &c.*' but his acquaintance with the world must be but superficial, who could think that statesmen in general merited the high character of friends of truth, or friends of the poor.

He had said before,

Along the lawn where scatter'd hamlets rose,
Unweildy wealth and cumb'rous pomp repose:

He says now,

———The man of wealth and pride,
Takes up a space that many poor supplied.

That the domain of the ancient Feudal Lord, or Rural Squire, was less exten-

five

five than that of the modern Peer, Place-
man, or Nabob, may be doubted; but
as many old manfions yet retain their
furrounding parks, warrens, &c. and
many new villas are erected, and adorned
with fpacious plantations; pleafure may
be juftly faid to have encroached on cultivation, and the rich to have remotely
abftracted from the provifion of the poor.
But the influx of foreign wealth has
been mifchievous in another point of
view: the new or commercial gentry
acquiring their money with eafe, have,
in verification of the proverb, ' *light*
' *come, light go,*' wantonly raifed the
price of commodities: the old, or land-
ed gentry, unwilling to defcend from
their ftate, and unable otherwife to fup-
port it, have been obliged to augment
the fize, and advance the rent of their
farms :* the great farmer has not been

* By augmenting the fize of farms, repairs are faved,
and rent is in general better paid. Whether the practice
is fo injurious to the community, as has been fuppofed,
is a point not eafy to determine.

injured

injured by his increased payment, for the increased value of his corn and cattle has enabled him to pay it, and often to become opulent. But there has been one sufferer; the little farmer has been annihilated, or at least metamorphosed into a labourer; and the labourer has had less work, the same wages, and more expence for necessaries. The Author of these remarks must confess, that when he has visited some of our capital seats, their seemingly interminable length of lawn, broken only by a few gloomy woods, has worn, to him, an air of melancholy solitude and idle waste, that was far from being agreeable. He has wished to exchange his situation for the vale of corn-clad inclosures, the winding lane, and shrub-hung brow, with their group of humble cottages, and chearful inhabitants. The possessors of these places are themselves sometimes not destitute of such feelings; the ingenious Mr. Potter, in his excellent Observati-

ons

ons on the Poor laws, has recorded a memorable inſtance of it : ‘ The late Earl ‘ of Leiceſter,’ ſays he, ‘ being compli- ‘ mented upon the completion of his ‘ great deſign at Holkham, replied,’ “ It “ is a melancholy thing to ſtand alone “ in one’s country. I look round ; not a “ houſe is to be ſeen but mine. I am the “ giant of giant-caſtle, and have eat up “ all my neighbours.” What then muſt be the caſe, when theſe faſhionable decorations are acquired by immediate rapine, extortion, or oppreſſion ; by the plunder of Hindoos, and the ſlavery of Negroes ? One is ready to aſk if it be poſſible to enjoy them.*

—In their towers raz’d villages I ſee,
And tears of orphans wat’ring every tree ;

* The proprietors of theſe improvements, as they are called, even if they are innocently obtained, ſeldom derive much ſatiſfaction from them. The pleaſure they afford chiefly reſults from making them ; when they are completed, few objects ſooner produce ſatiety :

Tir’d of the ſcenes parterres and fountains yield,
He finds at laſt he better likes a field. —Pope.

Are

Are thefe mock ruins that invade my view?
They are the entrails of the poor Gentoo;
That column's trophied bafe his bones fupply,
That lake the tears that fwell'd his fable eye.
                                    LANGHORNE.*

Goldfmith's laft quoted paffage, ' *Ye*
' *friends to truth, &c.*' has been confidered in a political view; fome attention muft now be given to its poetry.
' *Folly hailing,*' or welcoming, the fhips
to the fhore, is a noble perfonification.
The breaks in thefe lines, ' *Yet count our*
' *gains,*' ' *Not fo our lefs, &c.*' have rather a difagreeable efiect.   In blank verfe,
to continue the fenfe from one line to
another, is always more or lefs neceffary;
but in rhyme it is feldom advantageous.
The detached, or unconnected parts of
a verfe, unlefs very carefully managed,
are always profaifms. By this couplet,

The robe that wraps his limbs in *filken floth*,
Has robb'd the neighb'ring fields of half their
growth;

* See his COUNTRY JUSTICE. A Poem in which a
fine poetical fancy is united with juft fatire.

the poet undoubtedly meant to intimate, that a confiderable tract of land
would not produce more profit than was
requifite to defray the expence of a rich
man's clothing. Extravagance in drefs,
was perhaps more the foible of former
ages than of the prefent; but be this as it
may, the notion of a ' *robe robbing fields*
' *of their growth*,' is hyperbolical, aukward, and far-fetched. It might have
been more tolerable in a country of mul-
berry-trees. A juvenile writer would
doubtlefs think the phrafe of ' *wrapping*
' *limbs in filken floth*,' a grand ftroke,
conveying the combined ideas of finery
and lazinefs. ' *The feat fpurning the*
' *cottage from the green*,' would have
been a beautiful imperfonation; but the
effect of it is entirely deftroyed by the
context, ' *where folitary fports are feen:*'
the ' *Seat*,' confidered in itfelf, fancy
might readily convert into a ' *Perfon*;'
but the ' *feat where folitary fports are*
' *feen*,' muft inevitably be ' *a place*.'

Our

Our author ufes the word '*fports*,' till
it becomes almoft infufferable; he moftly means by it the ale-houfe amufements
of villagers: he here muft mean the field-
diverfions of their fuperiors. The four
lines, '*Around the world*, *&c.*' had better have been fuppreffed: the firft two
are introduced abruptly; the tranfition
is not very natural or eafy, from the
great man's park, feat, and equipage,
to the exportation of neceffaries, and·the
importation of luxuries: the laft two
have little merit in themfelves, '*A land*
'*all adorned for pleafure, in barren fplen-*
'*dour feebly waiting a fall*,' is but an uncouth kind of language:

V. 289. As fome fair female *unadorn'd and plain*,
    Secure to pleafe, while youth confirms her
      reign;
    Slights every borrow'd *charm* that drefs fup-
      plies,
    Nor fhares with art the triumph of her eyes:
    But when thofe *charms* are paft, for charms
      are frail,
    When *time advances*, and when lovers fail,
                   She

She then fhines forth folicitous to blefs,
In all the glaring impotence of drefs.
Thus fares the *land*, by luxury betray'd,
In nature's fimpleft *charms* at firft array'd ;
But verging to decline, its fplendors rife,
It's viftas ftrike, it's palaces furprize ;
While fcourg'd by famine, from the fmiling
  land
The mournful peafant leads his humble band ;
And while he finks, without one arm to fave,
The country blooms—a garden, and a grave.

The predilection of criticks, and indeed
of readers in general, in favour of the
fimile, as an effential conftituent of
poetry, is fo ftrong, that whoever thinks
lightly of it, will probably be deemed
a fort of literary heretick. That fimilies are fometimes employed to great
advantage, muft be readily allowed ; but
that they are far from being always advantageous, is certain. In the above
paffage, nature and art are contrafted in
two different fubjects. Some diftant
kind of refemblance may be fancied,
between a fine fafhionable lady, and a
country

country full of palaces and gardens; but the parallel, as Goldsmith has drawn it, is exceedingly defective. Ornament in the woman, is the effect of a deliberate systematical design to recommend herself, and please others; the country is incapable of such design; and even those who adorn it, scarcely think of rendering it pleasing to any but themselves. The emigration affair is ' here ' again hammered on the ear,' by repetition; it is indeed introduced like the burden of a song, at every opportunity. There is however a noble picture, in ' *Famine scourging the peasant from the* ' *land.*' Perhaps a writer has not a more difficult task than to know when he has said enough : ' *Famine scourges* ' *the peasant from the land;*' so far the thought, however ill-placed, is proper; but while he is ' *scourg'd away*,' he is very inconsistently represented as ' *leading his humble band with him.*' We have then other new and unnecessary ideas,

ideas; he is '*scourged away*,' and he
'*leads his band*;' and now he '*sinks*.'
We are not however to suppose, that he
literally sinks into the ocean, or into the
grave, but metaphorically,* into poverty or distress: and he sinks, '*without*
'*one arm to save*;' which is an awkward,
and almost ludicrous substitute for saying, that there is no person able or willing to relieve him. The '*Country*
'*blooming a garden and a grave*,' is
another absurdity: had the peasantry
been described, as perishing at home,
the expression would have been just; but
the country could not be the '*grave*
'*of those who had left it*.'

V. 305. Where then, alas, shall poverty reside,
    To scape the pressure of contiguous pride?
    If to some common's sunceless limits stray'd,
    He drives his flock to pick the scanty blade;

* The metaphor is an *ignis fatuus*, that leads many
a poet into the bog of nonsense: for instances of this,
recourse may be had to Dr. Young's Night Thoughts,
and to some productions of the present day.

Those

Those fenceless fields the fons of wealth divide,
And e'en the bare-worn common is deny'd.

The great fault of this Poem, is a difre-
gard to confiftency. The previous repeated hints of the emigration, had intirely fuperfeded the above paffage; for
thofe whom ' *Famine had fcourged from*
' *the land,*' it furely need not have been
afked, ' *in what part of it they fhould*
' *refide.*' With fimilar impropriety Rural Poverty, which we were led to fup-
pofe had left its native land, is now
introduced as retiring to the metropo-
lis; but is fhewn to derive no advantage from a retreat thither. ' The *glit-*
' *tering courtier,*' is there contrafted
with the ' *pale artift, who plies the fickly*
' *trade;*' and tumultuous Grandeur, and
her rattling chariots, glaring torches,
&c. with the diftrefsful fituation of a
poor proftitute, who

—Once perchance in village plenty bleft,
Has wept at tales of innocence diftreft:

Her

Her modeſt looks the cottage might adorn,
Sweet as the primroſe peeps beneath the thorn:
Now loſt to all her friends, her virtue fled,
Near her betrayer's door ſhe lays her head;
And pinch'd with cold, and ſhrinking from the
    ſhower,
With heavy heart deplores that luckleſs hour,
When idly firſt, ambitious of the town,
She left her wheel, and robes of country brown.

This is a fine paſſage: there is beauty in the ſimile of the primroſe, and pathos in the mention of the unhappy girl laying her head at the door of her betrayer; but the latter ſeems rather enfeebled by the addition of theſe lines, ' *With heavy* ' *heart, &c.*'

The Author now rather unſkilfully returns to his ſubject, by the following inquiry:

Do thine, *ſweet* Auburn, thine the lovelieſt
    train,
Do thy fair tribes participate her pain?
E'vn now perhaps by cold and hunger led,
At proud men's doors they aſk a *little bread.*

The

The reply to this query, introduces the emigration in full detail:

Ah no! to diſtant climes a dreary ſcene,
Where half the convex world intrudes between,
To torrid tracts, with fainting ſteps they go,
Where wild Altama murmurs to their woe:
Far different there from all that charm'd be-
    fore,
The various terrors of that horrid ſhore;
Thoſe blazing ſuns that dart a downward ray,
And fiercely ſhed intolerable day;
Thoſe matted woods, where birds forget to
    ſing,
But ſilent bats in drowſy cluſters cling;
Thoſe poiſonous fields, with rank luxuriance
    crown'd,
Where the dark ſcorpion gathers death around;
Where at each ſtep the ſtranger fears to wake
The rattling terrors of the vengeful ſnake;
Where crouding tigers wait their hapleſs prey,
And ſavage men more murderous ſtill than
    they;
While oft in whirl, the *mad* tornado flies,
Mingling the ravag'd landſcape with the ſkies.
Far different theſe from every former ſcene,
The cooling brook, the graſſy-veſted green,
The breezy covert of the warb'ling grove,
That only ſhelter'd thefts of harmleſs love.

This

This piece is animated, and in general correctly drawn; the candid rational critick can have little objection to it. The general effect of the passage is indeed weakened by the two last couplets, '*Far different, &c.*' which are totally superfluous, and of dissimilar character. The compound '*grassy-vest-ed*,' is a bad one; the adjective '*grassy*,' conveys the whole sense, consequently the participle, '*vested*,' is tautologous; grass-vested, or verdure-vested, would have been proper.

V. 367. Good heav'n! what sorrows gloom'd that parting day,
 That call'd them from their native walks away:
 When the poor exiles, every pleasure past,
 Hung round their bowers, and fondly look'd their last;
 And took a long farewell, and wish'd in vain,
 For seats like these beyond the western main;
 And shudd'ring still to face the distant deep,
 Return'd and wept, and still return'd to weep.
 The good old sire the first prepar'd to go,
 To new-found worlds, and wept for others woe;
   But

But for himself in conscious virtue brave,
He only wish'd for worlds beyond the grave.
His lovely daughter, lovelier in her tears,
The fond companion of his helpless years,
Silent went next, neglectful of her charms,
And left a lover's for a father's arms.
With *louder plaint*, the mother spoke her *woes*,
And blest the cot where *every pleasure rose*;
And kiss'd her thoughtless babes with many a
    tear,
And claspt them close, in sorrow doubly dear;
While her fond husband strove to lend relief,
In all the decent manliness of grief.

An injudicious arrangement is obvious here again. This passage should have preceeded the passage last quoted, ' *Ah no,* ' *to distant climes, &c.*' the people should have been introduced as going, before the place to which they were to go, had been described. This disposition would have produced another advantage, a climax in character, from the pathetick to the sublime. This paragraph has many beauties: the heart must be insensible indeed, which does not feel the force

T   of

of pathos, in the circumstances of the daughter relinquishing her lover, in order to attend her father; and the mother clasping her thoughtless babes, with additional tenderness. The *Labor limæ*, might however have been employed to advantage; the lines in italicks might have been spared; and the positive adjective, '*silent*,' in the 15th line, and the comparative, '*louder*,' in the 17th, do not agree :· to say that some *accents* are *louder* than others, is proper; but to say that any *accents* are *louder* than *silence*, is absurd, because *silence* cannot be '*loud*' at all. The idea of habitations had been conveyed under the name of '*bowers*,' the mention of them again, under the name of '*the cot where every pleasure rose*,' was needless. The expression, '*where every pleasure rose*,' is unusual, and rather aukward.

This is succeeded by an apostrophe to Luxury, in which kingdoms inebriated by her

her potions, are not very elegantly compared to an hydropic human body. This
apostrophe is ill placed, as it intercepts
the connection between the last quotation, ' *Good heaven, &c.*' and the following, which concludes the poem:

> Ev'n now the desolati⋯ ⋯oun,
> And half the business ⋯ ⋯ done;
> Ev'n now methinks, ⋯ ⋯g here I stand,
> I see the rural virtues leave the land.
> Down where yon anchoring vessel spreads the
>   sail,
> That idly waiting, flaps with every gale;
> Downward they move, a melancholy band,
> Pass from the shore, and darken all the strand.
> Contented toil, and hospitable care,
> And kind connubial tenderness are there;
> And piety with wishes plac'd above,
> And steady loyalty, and faithful love.
> And thou sweet Poetry, thou loveliest maid,
> Still first to fly where sensual joys invade,
> *Unfit in these degenerate times of shame,*
> *To catch the heart, and strike for honest fame;*
> Dear charming nymph, neglected and deny'd,
> My shame in crouds, my solitary pride!
> Thou source of all my bliss, and all my woe,
> Thou found'st me poor at first, and keep'st
>   me so;

Thou

Thou guide by which the nobler arts excell,
Thou nurse of every virtue, fare thee well!
Farewell—and O where'er thy voice be tried,
On Torno's cliffs, or Pambamarca's side;
Whether where equinoctial fervours glow,
Or winter wraps the polar world in snow;
Still let thy voice prevailing over time,
Redress the rigour of th'inclement clime;
Aid slighted truth with thy perswasive strain,
Teach erring man to spurn the rage of gain;
Teach him that states of native strength possest,
Though very poor, may yet be very blest;
That trade's proud empire hastes to swift decay,
As ocean sweeps the labour'd mole away;
While self-dependent power can time defy,
As rocks resist the billows and the sky.

This is a fine passage, but it would admit of improvement: the first couplet, ' *Even now, &c.*' is little better than an absurdity; the devastation is ' *begun,*' and ' *half done,*' at the same time. The connection with the preceeding quotation, would have been better, if those two lines had been omitted, and the third line had begun thus, ' *With them, &c.*' ' The *anchor'd vessel,*' with its ' *flapping* ' *sail,*'

' *fail*,' is a natural and beautiful image. The addrefs to Poetry has a noble enthufiafm, but wants correctnefs: the lines in italicks, ' *Unfit in thefe degene-* ' *rate, &c.*' might have been fpared; ' *Strike for honeft fame*,' is an unmeaning phrafe, nearly allied to nonfenfe; and what affinity the circumftance of the voice of Poetry ' *prevailing over time*,' can have with the circumftance of its ' *redreffing the rigour of a climate*,' is not obvious. I am not one of thofe who difcover even a cafual imitation in every refemblance; but poffibly the ideas of two former writers might have ' re- ' murmured' in our poet's ' memorial ' cell,' when he wrote thefe lines. Prefixed to Pope's works are feveral complimentary copies of verfes, in one of which, the author fpeaking of the ftory of Lodona, fays,

The foft complaint fhall over time prevail.

And Gray, in his progrefs of poetry, has the following :

T 3

In

In climes beyond the folar road,
Where fhaggy forms o'er ice-built mountains
  roam,
The mufe has broke the twilight gloom
  To chear the fhivering native's dull abode.

The Deferted village, as has been hinted, is, on the whole, a performance of great merit; it has numerous excellencies, and numerous faults; and while we are charmed with the former, we cannot but regret that more pains was not taken to avoid the latter.

T 3   ESSAY

ESSAY IX.

On Thomson's Seasons.

GENERAL Criticifm can fay little of the SEASONS, that has not been faid already. The ingenious Mr. Aikin, in the Effay prefixed to his edition, has explained their plan and character; and to Dr. Johnfon's opinion of them, there is no great reafon to object. Particular criticifm cannot be expected to purfue her tafk regularly, through a Poem of fuch length; but the examination of fome detached paffages, will perhaps fufficiently point out the nature of its beauties and defects.

Thomfon

Thomson obferved clofely, and defcribed forcibly. He feldom diftracts
the reader's attention by the introduction of heterogenous ideas; he has few
fimilies, and few allufions ; but he errs,
by endeavouring to imprefs his fubject
on the mind, with a pomp and redupli-
cation of expreffion. He often, in attempting energy and dignity, produces
bombaft and obfcurity ; and in avoiding
meannefs, becomes guilty of affectation.
His language is indeed a kind of anamo-
ly, for which he had no example, and
which it would not be eafy to imitate.

The country wears one of its moft
beautiful appearances, when the orchards
and hedges are in blofiom ; this he defcribes as follows :

—————————I purfue my walk,
And fee the country far-diffus'd around,
One boundlefs blufh, one *white-impurpled fhow.r*
Of mingled blofioms ; where the raptur'd eye

Hurries

Hurries from *joy* to *joy*, and hid beneath
The fair profusion, *yellow autumn* spies.

This passage gives a general confused idea of the subject, but they are extremely deficient in correctness. To term the country a ' *boundless blush*,' because it is covered with trees in bloom, however bold, is perhaps justifiable; but to term that country a ' *white empurpled shower*,' because the trees have shed their blossoms, is surely rather too violent. That the raptured eye hurried from place to place, might have been said properly; but to say it hurried from ' *joy*' to ' *joy*,' when nothing of *joy* had been previously mentioned, seems carrying figurative language almost to absurdity.* He who sees trees in bloom, must naturally suppose that they will bear fruit, and his imagination may behold them fraught with it; but his *eye* may look in vain among the

* The Author meant undoubtedly, the places or prospects that afforded *joy* or *pleasure*.

blossoms,

bloffoms, to *fpy* the poetical perfon *autumn.* There is befides fomething whim-
fical, if not ludicrous, in the fuppofed
concealment and difcovery of the imperfonated feafon.

Our poet's picture of the approach and
defcent of a ' *vernal fhower*,' is one of
his capital pieces. It is a fair fpecimen
of his general manner; its beauties and
defects are fo intermixed, that it is no
eafy matter to feparate them.

> ——————— Gradual finks the breeze
> Into a perfect calm; that not a breath,
> Is heard to quiver through the *clofing* woods,
> Or rufhing hum the *many-twinkling* * leaves
> Of afpin tall. The uncurling floods, diffus'd
> In glaffy breath, *feem through delufive lapfe*
> *Forgetful of their courfe.* 'Tis filence all,
> And pleafing expectation. Herds and flocks
> Drop the dry fprig, and *mute-imploring*, eye

* GRAY has been cenfured for the ufe of this compound *many-twinkling*, but his cenfurers have not remarked that Thomfon had ufed it before him.

T'e

The falling verdure. Hush'd in short suspense,
The plumy people *streak their wings with oil,*
To throw the *humid moisture* trickling off;
And wait the approaching sign to strike at once
Into the general choir. Ev'n mountains, vales,
And forests, *seem, impatient,* to demand
The *promis'd sweetness.* Man superior walks
Amid the glad creation, musing praise,
And looking lively gratitude. At last,
The clouds consign their treasures to the fields;
And softly-shaking on the dimpled pool,
Prelusive drops *let all their moisture flow,*
In large effusion o'er the freshen'd world.

There are here two kinds of circumstances, one actually existent in nature,
and one the product of the Poet's imagination. The calm is of the first sort,
and is forcibly expressed by the quief-
cence of the aspin, and the glaffinefs of
the water. The '*floods seeming forgetful*
'*of their course,*' is of the second, and
might be an allowable hyperbole; but
in the present cafe, it wants propriety.
A poetical mind too seldom thinks with
precision; imagination is apt to act
without

without judgment, and confound
object with another. The floods could
not seem '*forgetful of their course,*' for
their *course* was not stopped. On the
cessation of the wind, the curl or undu-
lation on the surface would cease, but
the motion of the current would not be
destroyed. When the gale sunk, a pool
would become smooth; but a river which
run before, would run still, and with
the same velocity.* To say that the
floods seem forgetful of their course,
'*through delusive lapse,*' is to talk nonsense. The '*birds and the flocks drop-
'*ping the dry sprig,*' may possibly be a
natural action; nor may it be deemed
too bold to represent them as '*implor-
'*ing the coming shower;*' but it is certainly too violent an anticipation to

* Thomson seems to have caught his idea from a very
gentle stream, which, in a calm, would appear totally
smooth; but even such a stream would have a *course*, or
current, which it consequently could not be properly said to *free*.

make

make them ' *eye or view that shower as*
' *falling*,' before it began to fall.   It is
also as violent a substitution of effect for
cause, to call the rain ' *verdure*;' and
worse still, by the addition of a previous
and totally inapplicable epithet, to term
it ' *falling verdure*.'   Fancy seems indeed here to have run wild; she supposes that the ' *herds*' implore the rain,
and at the same time see it ' *falling*;'
and *imagine* they *see* in it the *green colour*, which will, in consequence of it,
cover their future pastures.   How far
the affair of the birds moistening
their plumage with an oleaginous matter, or in our author's words, ' *streak-
' ing their wings with oil*,' is a fact, I
pretend not to determine.   The circumstance of the ' *mountains, forests, &c.
' seeming impatient for the rain*,' if not
too poetically bold, is at least misplaced ;
it should have immediately followed that
of ' *the rivers seeming forgetful of their
' course*; the process would then have been,
from

from inanimate to animate matter, from
water and earth, to birds, beasts, and man;
this would have been a climax. The
' *prelufive drops on the dimpled pool*,' is a
beautiful ftroke; but it was unneceffary
to fay, firft, that ' *The clouds confign their*
' *treafures to the fields*,'* and next, that
they ' *let all their moifture flow in large*
' *effufion o'er the frefhen'd world*.'

> The ftealing fhower is fcarce to *patter* heard,
> By fuch as wander through the foreft walks,
> Beneath the umbrageous multitude of leaves.
> But who can hold the fhade, when *heaven de-*
> *fcends*
> In univerfal bounty, *feedling herbs*
> *And fruits and flowers* on nature's ample lap?
> *Swift* fancy *fir'd*, anticipates their growth;
> And while the *mil'y nutriment* diftills,
> Beholds the *kindling* country *colour* round.

There is nature in the firft three lines of
the above, but an unnatural affectation

* This line, confidered in itfelf, has great merit. The
oppofition between the *clouds* and the *fields*, and the tranf-
miffion of the rain from the former to the latter, are ideas
well conceived and expreffed.

in

in the reft. Walking *under thick trees*
in a vernal rain, which does not pene-
trate, is certainly very pleafant; but
walking *abroad* even in fuch a rain,
would hardly be agreeable enough to
produce fine reveries on the profpect of
plenty. This paffage alfo is verbofe and
affected; ' *Fancy is fir'd, the country*
' *kindles, &c.*' the thought fimply expreffed, is this; that heaven in fhed-
ding the rain, fheds herbs and flowers;
&c. and that fancy anticipates their
growth, and beholds the country covered with them.

Where a fubject occupies any confiderable number of lines, it is commonly
neceffary to mention it repeatedly, either in the fame terms, or in others.
The permitting one word to recur frequently, has been juftly termed a flo-
venly practice; and writers, to avoid it,
often have recourfe to a kind of metonymical, or rather catachreftical expreffions,

preffions, which are moftly either improper or inelegant. Thomfon has a great
number of thefe quaint phrafes of his
own conftruction. The reader muft
have obferved, that in the two immediately preceding paffages, the fingle circumftance of rain, is defcribed by no
lefs than feven different appellations; it
is called ‘ *falling verdure*,’ ‘ *lucid moi-*
‘ *flure*,’ ‘ *promis’d fweetnefs*,’ ‘ *treafures*
‘ *of the clouds*,’ ‘ *heaven defcending in*
‘ *univerfal bounty*,’ ‘ *fruits and flowers*,’
and laftly, ‘ *milky nutriment.*’

> Thus all day long the full-diftended clouds,
> Indulge their genial ftores and well-fhower’d
>   earth
> Is *deep-enrich’d* with vegetable life;
> Till in the weftern fky the *downward fun*
> Looks out effulgent from *amid the flufh*
> Of broken clouds, gay-fhifting to his beam.
> The rapid radiance inftantaneous ftrikes;
> The illumin’d mountains through the foreft
>   ftreams,   .
> Shakes on the floods, and in a yellow mift
> Far fmoaking o’er the interminable plain,
> In twinkling myriads lights the dewy gems.
>   *Moift,*

Moist, *bright*, and *green*, the landscape *laughs*
  around ;
Full swell the woods, their every music wakes,
Mix'd in wild concert with the warbling brooks
Increas'd, the distant bleatings of the hills,
The *hollow lows* responsive from the vales,
Whence blending all the *sweeten'd* zephir
  springs.

That a mind fully poffeffed of its fubject,
fhould aim to exprefs it in every pof-
fible method, is natural ; confequently
one cannot wonder at finding in poetry,
fuch frequent reiteration of the fame
ideas in different expreffions. The writer may experience no difguft from this
redundance, but the reader muft ; for
he has conceived the thought, and wifhes
not to dwell upon it, but to quit it for
another. This is generally the cafe, but
not conftantly ; repetition fometimes
pleafes. Our author had defcanted large-
ly on his vernal rain ; but he introduces
it here again, ' *Thus all day long, &c.*'
with much dignity and eafe. This paf-

fage has great merit; nothing can be more natural and picturefque, than the images of the '*fun fhining* from among ' the *broken clouds*, and his *radiance ftrik-* ' *ing* on the *mountain*, *ftreaming* through ' the *foreft*, *trembling* on the *water*, ' *fmoaking* in the *yellow mift*, and *glitter-* ' *ing* on *the drops of rain*.' There is a confufion, and contrariety of ideas in the circumftance of the ' *landfcape laugh-* ' *ing :*' the verb ' *laugh*,'* rather indicates a poetical perfon ; but the epithets *round*, *moift*, *bright*, and *green*, are only compatible with a natural object. ' *Full* ' *fwell the woods*,' is an aukward phrafe, whofe meaning can fcarcely be dif- covered; and ' *Their every mufic wakes*,' is but little better. Thofe who are cu-

* The human countenance, when fmiling, is beheld with complacence ; and by a catachrefis, or inverfion, a fine profpect, which is agreeable to the eye, is faid to ' *fmile ;*' but the word ' *laugh*,' however authorized, is too ftrong, and muft convey a perfonal idea.

rious

rious in found, will be difgufted with the cacophony in ' *hollow lows.*' The ' *zephir*' may be properly faid to ' *blend*,' or mingle, the various noifes; but why that ' *zephir*' fhould be faid to ' *fpring*,' particularly ' *from the vales*,' and why it fhould be faid to be ' *fweet- en'd*,' are queftions which it is natural to afk, but poffibly they could not be eafily anfwered.

The amufement of angling has been generally regarded as a diverfion, not only inoffenfive in itfelf, but alfo favourable to the meditations of the phi-. lofophical and religious. Perhaps, however, it might be difficult to reconcile with the idea of moral rectitude, the idea of pleafure obtained by the punifhment of innocent beings.* The attention of

---

* This confideration apart, the amufement might be, in fome refpects, agreeable, and defcriptions of it generally pleafe; witnefs that engaging book, WALTON's Complete Angler, and Mr. MOSES BROWNE's truly poetical Pifcatory Eclogues.

an

an angler will also be too anxiously employed on the object he is endeavouring to procure, to admit the exercise
of his mental powers on diffimilar fubjects. Of this amufement, Thomfon
has given a defcription full of mafterly
ftrokes ; a defcription, which fhews that
he muft either have practifed it himfelf,
or attended very clofely on the practice
of it by others.

> Now when the firft foul torrent of the brooks,
> Swell'd with the vernal rains, is ebb'd away ;
> And whitening, down their maffy-tinctur'd
>   ftream
> Defcends the billowy foam ; now is the time,
> While yet the dark-brown water aids the guile,
> To tempt the trout. The well diffembled fly,
> The rod fine-tapering with elaftic fpring,
> Snatch'd from the hoary fteed the floating line,
> And all thy flender watery ftores prepare.

The proper feafon for the fport, and the
implements requifite for it, are here detailed with a moft ftriking particularity,
though not with the greateft correctnefs
of

of language. The compound ' *moſſy-*
' *tinctur'd,*' ſeems improperly introduced; one ſhould ſuppoſe it was deſigned
to convey the idea of a greeniſh colour,
but we are told, that the water is ' *dark-*
' *brown.*' ' *To tempt the trout,*' is pro-
ſaick. The ' *well-diſſembled fly,*' is ſimple and juſt; and the ' *rod fine tapering*
' *with elaſtic ſpring,*' is expreſſive; but
to have mentioned the ' *floating line,*'
would ſurely have been ſufficient, without intimating that it was made of white
horſe-hair; and that in a manner ſo obſcure, ' *Snatch'd from the hoary ſteed, &c.*'
that, if the circumſtance was not generally known, the verſe would be unintelligible. The next line is an ex-
creſcence; it is not eaſy to gueſs what
' *other ſlender watry ſtores,*' were intended for preparation.

> But let not on thy hook the tortur'd worm,
> Convulſive, twiſt in agonizing folds;
> Which by rapacious hunger ſwallow'd deep,
> Gives as you tear it from the bleeding breaſt

Of the weak helpless uncomplaining wretch,
Harsh pain, and horror to the tender hand.

The man of humanity, who reads this,
however fond of fishing he may be, will
surely never impale a worm again. The
picture is indeed drawn with such force,
as almost to shock imagination.

High to their fount, this day amid the hills,
And woodlands warbling round,† trace up the
    brooks;
The next purfue their rocky chancll'd maze
Down to the rivers, in whose ample wave
Their little naiads love to fport at large.
Juft in the dubious point, where with the pool
Is mix'd the tremb'ling ftream, or where it
    boils
Around the ftone, or from the hollow'd bank
Reverted plays in undulating flow,
There throw nice-judging the delufive fly;

† ‘ *Woodlands warbling round.*’ This is an inftance
of poetical boldnefs, without impropriety: the *woods*
are, without any great violence, fubftituted for the
birds who inhabit them.

                                    And

And as you lead it round in artful curve,
With eye-attentive mark the springing game.

The Poet has here described the places
proper for angling, with uncommon accuracy: our fancy is delighted with his
' *hills and woods,*' and ' *rocky channell'd*
' *brooks* ;' and a painter could not have
given a water scene, with all its minute
diversities, more exactly than he has in
his ' *pool mixing with the stream,*' and his
' *stream boiling around the stone,*' or ' *re-*
' *verted from the hollow bank.*'

> Strait as above the surface of the flood
> They wanton rise, or urg'd by hunger leap,
> Then fix, with gentle twitch, the barbed
>   hook :
> Some lightly-tossing to the grassy bank,
> And to the shelving shore slow-dragging some,
> With various hand proportion'd to their force.

The motions of the fish, and the operations of the angler, are here detailed
with wonderful precision. The com-

pound

pound epithets, ' *lightly toffing*,' ' *flow-*
' *dragging*,' are ftrikingly expreffive of
the actions; but fome may think them
wanting in poetical dignity.

> If yet too young, and eafily deceiv'd,
> A worthlefs prey fcarce bends your pliant rod,
> Him *piteous of his youth, and the firft fpace*
> *He has enjoy'd the vital light of heaven,*
> Soft difengage, and back into the ftream
> The *fpeckled infant* throw.*

The praife beftowed on the preceding
paffage, cannot be juftly given to this.
There is in it an attempt at dignity above
the occafion.   Pathos feems to have been
intended, but affectation only is produced.

> —————————— But fhould you lure
> From his dark haunts, beneath the tangled
> roots
> Of pendent trees, the monarch of the brook,

---

* The paffage ftands thus in fome of the common editions.   Mr. AIKIN reads ' *fpeckled captive*.'

Behoves

Behoves you then to ply your finest art.
Longtime he following cautious, scans the fly,
And oft attempts to seize it; but as oft
The dimpled water speaks his jealous fear.
At laft while haply o'er the fhaded fun
Paffes a cloud, he defperate takes *the death*
With fullen plunge. At once he darts along,
Deep-ftruck, and runs out all the lengthen'd
    line;
Then feeks the fartheft ooze, the fheltering weed,
The cavern'd bank, his old fecure abode;
And flies aloft, and flounces round the pool,
Indignant of the guile. With yielding hand
That feels him ftill, yet to his furious courfe
Gives way, you, now retiring, following now
Acrofs the ftream, exhauft his idle rage:
Till floating broad upon his breathlefs fide,
And to his fate abandon'd, to the fhore
You *gaily* drag your unrefifting prize.

This is a remarkable inftance of that
poetry, which can " turn readers into
" fpectators." The whole procefs of
catching a large fifh, is defcribed in the
moft explicit and judicious manner;
but the language is in fome few inftances
exceptionable.

Thomfon's

Thomson's account of the different situations, chosen by different birds for their nests, demonstrates the closest observations of nature; but the language has his usual inequality:

> ——— ———Some to the holly hedge
> *Nestling* repair, and to the thickset some;
> Some to the rude protection of the thorn
> Commit their feeble offspring. The cleft tree
> Offers its kind concealment to a few,
> Their food its insects, and its moss their nests.
> Others apart far in the grassy dale,
> Or *roughening waste* their *humble texture*
> weave.
> But most in woodland solitudes delight,
> In unfrequented glooms, or shady banks,
> Steep, and divided by a bubbling brook,
> Whose murmurs sooth them all the livelong
> day,
> When by kind duty fix'd. Among the roots
> Of hazel, pendent o'er the plaintive stream,
> They frame the first foundation of their *domes*;
> Dry sprigs of trees in artful fabrick laid,
> And bound with clay together. Now 'tis
> nought
> But restless hurry through the busy air,
>
> 　　　　　　　　　　　　　　　Best

Beat by unnumber'd wings. The swallow
  sweeps
The slimy pool, to build his hanging house
Intent.   And often from the *careless* backs
Of herds and flocks, a thousand tugging bills,
Pluck hair and wool; and oft, when unobserv'd,
Steal from the barn a straw : till soft and warm,
Clean, and complete, their habitation grows.

Some Criticks have supposed, that poetry can only deal in generals; or in other words, that it cannot subsist with any very minute specification of particulars. To such, this passage might be well produced as a proof, that their opinion is erroneous. That poetical power, which, in Homer, transports us to the banks of Simois, and shews us the shield of Achilles, or the casque of Hector; and in Virgil, sets before us the herdsman, ' who feebly dragg'd his goat along;' the vine-pruner singing at his labour upon the rocks, and even the smoaky rafters of a cottage; that power here conveys us to the woodland's remotest recesses,

recesses, among the shaggy banks, and hazel roots, projecting over the gurgling rills, where the feather'd race are building their habitations. The notation of time is always pleasing; there is something finely romantick in the idea of the birds being foothed with the murmurs of the brook ' *all the livelong* ' *day.*' The whole, however, concludes with an anticlimax: when we are told of ' *stealing from the barn a straw,*' however natural may be the action described by that expression, the expression itself is a wretched prosaism. ' *Clean and com-* ' *plete,*' also, is little better than ' clean ' and tight;' the diction of a house-maid or a char-woman.

The description of Hagley Park, and its profpects, has a remarkable mixture of beauties and faults:

O Lyttleton, the friend! *thy* paffions thus
And meditations vary, as *at large*

Courting the Muse, through Hagley Park you
  stray
Thy British Tempe! there along the dale,
With woods o'erhung, and shagg'd with mossy
  rocks,
Whence on each hand the gushing waters play,
Or down the rough cascade white-dashing fall,
Or gleam in lengthen'd vista through the trees,
You silent *steal*; or sit beneath the shade
Of solemn oaks, that tuft the swelling mounts,
Thrown graceful round by nature's careless
  hand,
And pensive listen to the various voice
Of rural peace: the herds, the flocks, the birds;
The hollow-whisp'ring breeze, the plaint of rills,
That purling down amid the twisted roots
That creep around, their *dewy murmurs stole*
On the sooth'd ear.——

This picture, though generally descrip-
tive, is not locally peculiar. Many or-
namented grounds have their ' *dales*
' *overhung with woods*,' and ' *shagged*
' *with rocks*;' their *swelling mounts*
crown'd with oaks, and *their waters*
falling in foamy cascades, or *shining* in
perspective among the trees. That com-
                                        mon

mon blemish in poetry, a change of person from singular to plural, and *vice versa*,
is here very disagreeably instanced;
' *Thy passions —you stray—thy British*
' *Tempe, &c.*' The language should have
been uniform, '*Your passions—you stray,—*
' *&c.*' ' The *various voice of rural peace*,'
is highly exceptionable : Peace and
noise are contradictory ideas. *Peace*
seems here to be personified, and a de-
ficiency of judgment is strikingly be-
trayed, in attributing to her a ' *voice so*
' *various*,' as the ' *lowing of herds*,' the
' *bleating of flocks*,' and the ' *sound of*
' *winds and waters*.' To call the gurgling of rills a ' *plaint*,' is boldly poetical ; but to call it in the same sentence,
' *dewy murmurs*,' is a redundancy.
' *Dewy murmurs*,' is a vicious expression :
the epithet ' *dewy*,' can relate only to
an object of feeling or sight, consequently it is absurdly joined with '*murmurs*,'
an object only of hearing .

Mean time

Mean time you gain the height from whose
   fair brow,
The bursting prospect spreads immense around:
And *snatch'd* o'er hill and dale, and wood and
   lawn,
And verdant field, and dark'ning heath be-
   tween,
And villages embosom'd soft in trees, *
And spiry towns by surging columns mark'd
Of houshold smoke, *your eye excursive reams :*
Wide stretching from the hall, *in whose kind
   haunt*
The hospitable Genius lingers still,
To where the broken landscape, by degrees,
Ascending, roughens into rigid hills ;
O'er which the Cambrian mountains, like far
   clouds
That skirt the blue horizon, dusky rise. †

  * Milton first introduced this beautiful image :

     Towers and battlements it sees,
     Bosom'd deep in tufted trees.

  † The Author of these observations was once on the
hill behind Hagley Park, and viewed this prospect. Perhaps few places in our own country, afford such a noble
assemblage of natural objects ; among others, the sublime convex of the Wrekin, and the enormous rocky
                         wall

This defcription has great force. To a perfon who has not feen the view it defcribes, it will convey a general, grand, and pleafing idea; to one who has feen that view, it will inftantly recall its particular beauties. But the language is here again incorrect. ' *Snatch'd,*' is fuperfluous and abfurd; for who would talk of ' *fnatching an eye?*'* It is alfo

placed

---

wall of Malvern, with great part of the counties of Salop, Worcefter, and Hereford, &c. beneath them. The day was cloudy, and he could not for fome time diftinguifh the Welch mountains from the clouds. He knew that fcenes of this kind are not to be feen in an inftant; and continued looking at the point he was directed to, through a good telefcope: while all near hand remained unillumined, the fun broke out at an immenfe diftance; objects, before in confufion, became diftinct and beautiful; he faw the mountains in their various pofitions, fhapes, and colours, glowing with brightnefs, and was ready to fancy them the regions of another world.

* It is a circumftance that cannot have efcaped notice, that moft authors have their favourite words, which they are apt to introduce too often. There feems a natural

tural

placed at such a distance from the verb
' roams,' with which it must connect,
in order to save the period from being
nonsense; that the reader at first does
not perceive the connexion. The adjective ' excursive,' and the compound,
' wide-stretching,' are also supernumera-
ries. The sentence placed in its natural order, will read thus: ' Your eye
' snatch'd over hill and dale, &c. roams
' excursive, wide-stretching from, &c.'
Blank verse, where such violent trans-
positions and unnecessary epithets are
used, surely is not unjustly accused of
obscurity. The ' kind haunt' of the

tural inclination to commit this fault, and I have perhaps
sometimes committed it myself, though it has disgust-
ed me in the works of others. I have already remarked, that GOLDSMITH, in his Deserted Village, has
used the substantive, ' Spots,' and the adjective, ' sweet,'
to an excess. Thomson seemed to have a predilection for
this word ' snatch'd;' his fishing line is ' snatch'd from the
' watery bed.' Spring, line 384, has been noticed; and
in line 516, he talks of ' snatching a hurried eye through
' a verdant maze.' He once uses it properly: The k si
' snatch'd hasty from the sidelong maid.' Winter, l. 625.

hall, is a needlefs periphrafis; it was fufficient to fay of the hall, that the ' *bofpitable genius*' lingered in it.

The defcription of Hay-making demands particular attention :

V. 331. Now fwarms the village o'er the jovial mead:
The ruftic youth brown with meridian toil,
Healthful and ftrong ; *full* as the fummer rofe
Blown by prevailing funs, the ruddy maid,
Half naked, fwelling on the fight, and all
Her kindled graces burning o'er her cheek.
Ev'n ftoop'g age is here ; and infant hands
Trail the long rake, or with the fragrant load
O'er charg'd amid the *kind oppreffion* roll.
Wide flies the *tedded grain* ; all in a row
Advancing broad, or wheeling round the field,
They fpread the breathing harveft to the fun,
That throws refrefhing round a rural fmell :
Or as they rake the green-appearing ground,
And drive the *dufky wave* along the mead,
The ruffet haycock rifes thick behind
In order gay.———•

Thomfon

• The reader may compare with the above, Doo-
.....'s defcription of the fame fubject, in his Poem,
called

Thomson was fond of delineating the female form, and he sometimes delineated it to advantage; but surely his ruddy hay-maker is described with more pomp than precision. The simile of the *Rose*, (of which, by the way, I do not perceive the propriety,) in the anticipatory manner in which it is introduced, renders the sentence obscure. ‘ *Swelling on the sight,* ’ is an expression either unmeaning, or indelicate; and a

called Publick Virtue, a work of very considerable poetical merit.

> —————In slanting rows,
> With still approaching step and levell’d stroke,
> The early mower bending o’er his scythe
> Lays low the slender grass, emblem of man
> Falling beneath the ruthless hand of time.
> Then follows blithe, equipt with fork and rake,
> In light array, the train of nymphs and swains.
> Wide o’er the field, their labour seeming sport,
> They toss the withering herbage; light it flies,
> Borne on the wings of zephir, whose soft gale,
> Now while the ascending sun’s bright beam exhales
> The grateful sweetness of the new-mown hay,
> Breathing refreshment, fans the toiling swain.

healthy

healthy countenance flufhed with heat and labour, is fomewhat ftrangely characterized by the term of *' kindled graces ' burning o'er a cheek.'* Our author has alfo here a whole group of his new-coined denominations; the hay is fucceffively called *' fragrant load, kind op-' preffion, tedded grain, breathing harveft, ' and dufky wave.'* *' Kind oppreffion,'* is a phrafe of that fort, which one fcarcely knows whether to blame, or praife: it confifts of two words, directly oppofite in their fignification; and yet, perhaps, no phrafe whatever could have better conveyed the idea of an eafy uninjurious weight.‡ *' Tedded grain,'* feems an unjuftifiable novelty; the grain,

l, as an important part of corn, is ten ufed for the *whole*; but is too unimportant a *part* of grafs, to be ufed

‡ The paffage however is highly redundant, *' With the fragrant load o'ercharg'd amid the kind op-' preffion rill.'*

for

for that in like manner: ' *Tedded*
' *grass*' would have been unexceptionable. ' *Dusky-wave*,' is bold, but not
improper; a resemblance is easily con-
ceiveable between rows of grass on a
plain, and ridges of water on the surface of the ocean. There is an ambiguity in this, ' *They spread the breath-*
' *ing harvest*, &c.' We know not whether it is meant, that the *sun*, by its ex-
haling power, throws the *refreshful smell*,
or whether it is meant that the hay itself threw it; if the latter was meant,
sense and grammar are at variance, as
sun is the substantive immediately connected with the verb *throws*. The circumstances of age unequal to harder labour, attending the comparatively lighter task of hay-making; of the children
trailing the rake, and rolling among the
swarths, and of the green appearing
ground, and russet haycock rising behind, are all equally just and beautiful.

X 3   From

From hay-making, the poet makes an abrupt transition to another pleasing rural occupation, viz. sheep-shearing :

Or rushing thence in one *diffusive land,*
They drive the troubled flocks, by many a *dog*
Compell'd, to where the mazy-running brook
Forms a deep pool : this bank abrupt and high,
And that fair-spreading in a pebbled shore.
Urg'd to the giddy brink, much is the toil,
The clamour much of men, and boys, and *dogs,*
E're the *soft fearful people,* to the flood
Commit their *woolly sides* ; and oft the swain
On some impatient seizing hurls them in :
Embolden'd then, nor hesitating more,
Fast, fast, they plunge amid the flashing wave,
And panting labour to the further shore.
Repeated this, till deep the well-wash'd fleece
Has drunk the flood, *and from his lively haunt*
The trout is banish'd by the sordid stream :
Heavy, and dripping, to the breezy brow
Slow move the harmless race ; where as they
      spread
Their *swelling treasures* to the sunny ray,
Inly disturb'd, and wond'ring what this wild
Outrageous tumult means, their loud com-
      plaints
The country fill, and *toss'd from* rock to rock,
Inceffant bleatings run around the hills.

                                            A:

At lyp, of snowy white, the gather'd flocks,
Are in the wattled pen innumerous pref's'd,
Head above head; and rang'd in lofty rows,
The shepherds sit, and whet the sounding
    shears.

The housewife waits to roll her fleecy stores,
With all her gay-dress'd maids attending round:
One, chief in gracious dignity enthron'd,
Shines o'er the rest, the pastoral queen, and
    rays

Her smiles *sweet beaming* on her shepherd king;
While the glad circle round them yield their
    souls

To festive mirth, and wit that knows no gall.
Mean time their joyous task goes on apace:
Some *mingling* stir the melted tar, and some
Deep on the new-shorn *vagrant's* heaving side,
To stamp their master's cypher ready stand;
Others th' unwilling weather drag along;
And glorying in his might, the sturdy boy
Holds by the twisted horns th'indignant ram. *

There

---

* Another parallel passage from DODSLEY's Publick
Virtue, may perhaps be not unacceptable. THOMSON
seems to have been kept in view, but not servilely imi-
tated. DODSLEY has adhered most closely to fact, in
marking a considerable interval of time between was
and shearing the sheep:

X 4

There is a total want of *vrai-semblance*, in the notion of a confused multitude rushing at once from the hay-field to the sheep-shearing: the expression, ' *diffu-* ' *five band,*' is an incongruity; ' *diffu-* ' *five,*' or ' *diffused,*' gives the idea of dispersion; ' *band,*' gives the idea of connection; diffusive train, or diffusive throng, would have been less exceptionable. There is a fine sketch of landscape in the washing-place, with one bank abrupt and high, the other

> ——————————Now beneath the sun,
> Mellowing their fleeces for th'impending sheers,
> The *woolly people*, in full clothing *sweat*,
> When the smooth current of a limpid brook,
> The shepherd seeks, and plunging in its waves
> The frighted innocents, their whitening robes
> In the clear stream grow pure. Emerging hence
> On litter'd straw, the bleating flocks recline;
> Till glowing heat shall dry, and breathing dews
> Perspiring soft, again through all the fleece
> Diffuse their *oily fatness*. Then the swain
> Prepares th' elastic shears, and gently down
> The patient creature lays; divesting soon
> Its lengthen'd limbs of their encumbering load.

spreading

spreading in a pebbled shore. For want of a previous substantive, the participle ' *urg'd*,' seems to stand looking about for something to concord with, and is ready to fall into the vacuity of no meaning. The Poet, at first sight, appears to have written nonsense, and said that ' *the toil and clamour of the men and dogs was much urged to the giddy brink.*' The passage may be read in this manner, ' *Much is the toil and clamour of men and dogs, before the soft fearful people commit their woolly sides to the flood:*' but it was probably intended thus, ' *When the flocks are urg'd to the giddy brink, much is the toil and clamour, &c. before they commit themselves to the water.*' The mention of ' *dogs*,' twice, was superfluous; it might have been easily avoided:

They drive the flocks to where the winding
    stream
Forms a deep pool, this bank abrupt and high, &c.

                    The

The phrases of '*soft fearful people,*' '*woolly sides, &c.*' have the character of affectation, and almost of burlesque. The following circumstances are strictly natural, and the sense is conveyed with the advantage of correspondent sound :

> ————————The swain,
> On some impatient seizing hurls them in :
> Embolden'd then, nor hesitating more,
> Fast, fast, they plunge amid the flushing wave,
> And panting, labour to the further shore.

When a writer's memory collects a number of different images, great judgment is required to decide what to retain, and what to reject. The mention of the '*muddy water banishing the trout* '*from his haunt,*' though perhaps matter of fact, is an extraneous affair, forcibly introduced, and interfering with the principal subject. We have a beautiful picture in the '*dripping flocks* '*moving to the breezy brow, and stand-* '*ing to dry in the sun;*' and an equally
striking

striking reprefentation of fact in the ' *inceffant bleatings echo'd from the hills.*' The expreffion might indeed have been more fimple; ' *fwelling treafures,*' might have been changed for ' *fwelling fleeces,*' and the ' *loud complaints,*' fhould have been rejected, as being the fame with the ' *inceffant bleatings.*' The tranfpofition is too bold in this line, ' *At laft,* ' *of fnowy white the gather'd flocks.*' The paftoral queen makes a very agreeable figure; but it is ftrange the author did not obferve the identity of fenfe in his verb ' *rays,*' and his compound, ' *fweet* ' *beaming :*' ' *fhe rays her fmiles fweet* ' *beaming,*' that is, ' *fhe beams her fmiles* ' *fweet beaming.*' The confinement of the fheep in the pens; the fhepherds wetting their fhears; the heaving of the fheep's fide under the operation of marking, and the boy holding the ram by the horns, are all fine minutiæ.*

The

* Our late celebrated landfcape painter, George Smith, of Chichefter, painted a piece called the Hay-Makers, another

The line, ' *some mingling stir, &c.*' is
prosaic. The phrase, ' *new-shorn vag-*
' *rant,*' is quaint; there is nothing relative to the subject that can require, or
even justify the word vagrant, and oc-
curring on such an occasion as that of
branding sheep, it becomes ludicrous,
as recalling the idea of burning a male-
factor in the hand.

That Thomson, in describing familiar
subjects, too often produced bombast
on one hand, or meanness on the other,
has been sufficiently shewn. The preceding quotations, with all their merit,

---

another called the Hop-Pickers, and another called the
Apple-Gatherers, but I do not recollect that he painted
a Sheep-Shearing: THOMSON's description would have
afforded him many fine hints. It is somewhat remarkable, that THOMSON has not described Hop-Picking,
or Apple-Gathering, though both might have been introduced with propriety in his Autumn. PHILIPS, in
his Cyder, has omitted Apple-Gathering, though so
important a part of his subject. The author of these
Essays has given a short occasional sketch of it in one
of his Eclogues. See his Poetical Works, p. 115.

cannot

cannot any of them be said to be thoroughly correct. Sometimes however he defcribed, with equal precifion, fimplicity, and dignity. Among other inftances of this kind may be ranked, his defcription of fwimming:

——————————The fprightly youth
Speeds to the well known pool, whofe chryftal
   depth
A fandy bottom fhows.   Awhile he ftands
Gazing the inverted landfcape, half afraid
To meditate the blue profound below ;
Then plunges headlong down the circling flood.
His ebon treffes, and his rofy cheek,
Inftant emerge ; and through th' obedient wave,
At each fhort breathing by his lip repell'd,
With arms and legs, according well he makes,
As humour leads, an eafy-winding path ;
While from his polifh'd fides a dewy light
Effufes on the pleas'd fpectators round.

The nut-gathering fcene in the Autumn, has equal exactnefs. Englifh poetry can boaft few paffages of fuperior beauty :

Ye

Ye swains now haften to the hazel bank,
Where down the dale the wildly-winding brook
Falls hoarse from steep to steep. In close array,
Fit for the thickets and the tangling shrub,
Ye virgins come. For you their lateft song
The woodlands raife; the cluftering nuts for you
The lover finds amid the fecret shade;
And where they burnish on the topmoft bough,
With active vigour crushes down the tree;
Or shakes them ripe from the refigning hufk,
A glossy flower, and of an ardent brown,
As are the ringlets of Melinda's hair.*

When Thomfon quits his rural fcenes for politer fubjects, his compofition has the fame variety of character. The Poet's enumeration of female accomplifhments, is one of thofe paffages which will pleafe in fpite of great incorrectnefs. Perhaps no man but himfelf could have written fuch a piece of beautiful and mellifluous abfurdity:

* The defcription of the red-breaft feeking fhelter in a cottage, is another inftance; it has the clofeft adherence to nature, but the language, though correct, is a lower ftrain.

—In

—In them 'tis graceful to diffolve at woe;
With every motion, every word, to wave
Quick o'er the *kindling cheek* the *ready* blush;
And from the fmalleft violence to fhrink
Unequal, then the lovelieft in their fears;
And by this filent adulation, foft,
To their protection more engaging man.

The tendernefs which fympathizes with diftrefs, the delicacy which blufhes at impropriety, and the timidity which is alarmed at violence, are here moft properly introduced; but they would have appeared to more advantage, if fome of the lines, in which they are defcribed, had been more concife and fimple:

—————————May their tender limbs
Float in the *loofe fimplicity* of drefs!
And, *fafhion'd all to harmony*, alone
Know they to *feize the captivated foul*
In *rapture*, warbling from love-breathing lips.
To teach the lute to languifh; *with fmooth ftep*
Difclofing motion in its every charm,
To fwim along, and *fwell* the mazy dance;
To train the foliage o'er the fnowy lawn;
To guide the pencil, turn the tuneful page,

To

To lend new flavour to the fruitful year,
And heighten nature's dainties; in their race
To rear their graces into second life,
To give society its highest taste.

Drefs, elegant and plain, is fo becom-
ing, that every lover of the Fair mufl
wifh to recommend it; but few would
think of recommending it, by talking of
' *limbs floating in a loofe fimplicity.*' The
knowledge of mufick is a moft engaging qualification, but the practifers of it
are not the moft perfpicuoufly characterized, by faying, that they are, or fhould
be, ' *fafhioned all to harmony.*' They
might have been very properly wifhed
to ' *feize or captivate the foul with melo-*
' *dy, warbled from love-breathing lips ;*'
but they are here wifhed, to ' *feize*' it
at the fame time that it is ' *captivated,*'
and to ' *feize*' it ' *in rapture.*'* Teach-

---

* Rapture is here fubftituted for vocal mufick; the
thing *caufed*, for the thing *caufing*. The poet however
fhould have faid ' *with rapture,*' not ' *in rapture.*'

ing

'ing *the lute to languish*,' is a fine poetical alternative for causing it to produce a languishing sound. Dancing may, without breach of propriety, be said to ' *disclose motion in its every charm*,' for motion is agreeable, and consequently may be said to have charms; but to ' *swim* ' *along with smooth step*,' is tautology; and how a ' *dance*,' especially a ' *mazy* ' *dance*,' could be ' *swelled*,' is not easy to explain. We can only guess what the author meant, by ' *lending new fla-* ' *vour to the fruitful year*;'* but surely his diction is above his subject, if he meant the making of sweetmeats, conserves, and pickles.‡ The context is

---

* The year is put for the fruit it produces. The ancients were fond of this metonymical expression; even the correct VIRGIL, (Eclog. I.) talks of *aristas*, beards, or ears of corn, for years. This manner might suit the genius of those times, but it is seldom used by modern writers to advantage.

‡ The operation is here heterogeneous to the subject, in order to *lend flavour* to the year, the year must be supposed capable of being eaten.

still

ftill more enigmatical, and equally tumid; a mother who, inftead of being advifed to nurfe and educate her children her-felf, fhould be advifed to ' *rear her gra-* ' *ces into fecond life,*' would fcarcely com-prehend the advifer's intentions.

When our author's fubject required a lofty ftrain: when he was relating cir-cumftances of diftrefs, or defcribing the grand phænomena of nature; we find fewer of his quaint new-coined phrafes, and ill-conftructed compounds; but he has other unfuccefsful efforts to elevate his diction; he is often turgid, often ob-fcure, and often redundant.

The ftory of Celadon and Amelia has great merit; but might have been told with more concifenefs, more fimplicity, and equal pathos:

> ————————————Young Celadon
> And his Amelia were a matchlefs pair;
> With equal virtue form'd, and equal grace,
> The fame, diftinguifh'd by their fex alone:
>
> Her's

Her's the mild luftre of the blooming morn,
And his the radiance of the rifen day.

This is a beautiful paffage: there is perhaps no finer inftance of attributive allufion in our language. The difference between mafculine and feminine beauty, is ftrikingly illuftrated by the difference between the ardour of the day, and the mildnefs of the morning.

They lov'd. But fuch their *guiltlefs* paffion was,
As in the dawn of time inform'd the *heart*
Of innocence, and undiffem'bling truth.

Figurative and circumlocutary expreffions have rendered thefe lines an enigma, for which many readers have probably ftood in need of an interpreter.*
The meaning in plain Englifh is this;
That the paffion of Celadon and Amelia

* There is a perverfe tendency in men to admire what they do not underftand. Not only hearers, but readers, are then beft pleafed with nonfenfe. This paffage has repeatedly been thought very fine by many who knew no meaning.

was

was guiltless as the passion of lovers in the dawn, that is to say, *in the earliest period of time.** When however this passion had been said *positively* to be guiltless, it was somewhat superfluous to say *comparatively*, that it was *guiltless* as that which informed the heart of the poetical person *innocence*; and it must be still greater tautology to say that it was *guiltless*, as that which informed the heart of another fictitious personage, *undissembling truth*. If it was *without guile*, it must be *innocent*; and if it was *innocent*, it must be *undissembling*; and if it was *undissembling*, it must be *true*.

> —— 'Twas friendship heighten'd by the mutual wish,
> The enchanting hope, and sympathetic glow,
> Beam'd from the mutual eye. *Devoting all*
> *To love, each was to each a dearer self*;

* What the Poet meant by this indeterminate expression, ' *dawn of time*,' is not easy to tell: was it the paradisaical state of innocence, or the fabulous golden age?

Supremely

Supremely happy in the awaken'd power
Of giving joy. Alone, amid the shades,
Still in harmonious intercourse they liv'd
The rural day, and talk'd the flowing heart,
Or sigh'd and look'd unutterable things.

Had the lines, ' *Devoting all, &c.*' been omitted, perhaps some advantage would have been derived from the omission. ' *To talk the flowing heart,*' for ' *talk-* ' *ing the sentiments flowing from the* ' *heart,*' is a bold ellipsis, but it will not incur the censure of the candid critick; and that forcible expression, ' *Or sigh'd* ' *and look'd, &c.*' must ensure his praise.

So pass'd their life, *a clear united stream,*
By care unruffled; till in evil hour
The tempest caught them on the tender walk,
Heedless how far, and where its mazes stray'd,
While, with each other blest, creative love
Still bade *eternal* Eden smile around.

Considering how amply the felicity of the lovers had been before insisted on, the mention that their life was ' *unruffled* ' *by care,*' is rather an anticlimax. This

same

same circumstance seems also again unnecessarily adverted to here ; ' *While with*
' *each other blest, &c.*' Some may indeed think this reiterated idea of pleasure
beauti.... as an immediate contrast to
the sub.....ent distress, but with me the
matter is doubtful. Criticism descends
to her lowest task, when she objects to
single words ; but that task is often useful. The phrase, ' *united streams*,' would
have been proper language, but the propriety of a ' *on united stream*,' is somewhat disputable. It was surely also a
glaring oversight, to call a momentary
scene of delight an ' *eternal*' Eden.

> Heavy with instant fate her bosom heav'd
> Unwonted sighs, and stealing oft a look
> Of the big gloom, on Celadon her eye
> Fell tearful, wetting her disorder'd cheek.
> In vain assuring love, and confidence
> In heav'n, repress'd her fear ; it grew and shook
> Her frame *near dissolution.*——

The progress of fear is here strikingly painted. Amelia's watching the approach of the storm, first weeping, and
then

then trembling, are a fine gradation of
natural circumſtances. The words ‘ *near*
‘ *diſſolution*,’ are, however, ſuperfluous;
if they mean that the terror alone had
nearly deſtroyed her frame, they are too
hyperbolical; if they mean ſimply, that
her death was near, they are improper,
as anticipating the cataſtrophe.

> ——————He perceiv’d
> Th’ unequal conflict, and as angels look
> On dying ſaints, his eyes compaſſion ſhed,
> With love illumin’d high. ‘ Fear not, he ſaid,’
> Sweet innocence! *the ſtranger to offence*,
> *And inward ſtorm!* He who yon ſkies involve,
> In frowns of darkneſs, ever ſmiles on thee
> With kind regard. O’er thee *the ſecret ſhaft*
> *That waſtes at midnight*, or *the undreaded hour*
> *Of noon, flies harmleſs:* and that very voice
> Which thunders terror through the guilty heart,
> With tongues of ſeraphs whiſpers peace to thine.
> ’Tis ſafety to be near thee, ſure, and thus
> To claſp perfection.——

The narrative manner in poetry ſucceeds
more frequently than the dramatick; we
can deſcribe action that we ourſelves
have ſeen, better than we can ſuppoſe

Y 4 what

what another would think or say on this or that occasion. The present passage is an instance in point. Celadon's behaviour is finely painted: the simile of angels looking on a dying saint, is in particular beautiful and appropriate; but his speech is unnaturally tedious and full of puerile confusion. The lightning which was, or should have been the immediate and sole object of notice, could not be, with any propriety, termed a ' *secret*' shaft; nor is there any meaning in talking of its ' *wasting at midnight,* ' *or the undreaded hour of noon.*'* How the very voice which ' *thundered terror,*' could at the same time ' *whisper peace,*' and ' *whisper it with tongues of seraphs,*' is not easy to comprehend. Should it be said in vindication of the Poet, that the voice was not meant to be represented as

* The Poet seems here to have improperly transferred the scriptural description of the pestilence, to his lightning. If he meant to introduce the pestilence, he wanted judgment; for the idea is evidently misplaced.

actually

actually of fuch inconfiſtent characters, but only fuppoſed to produce different effects on different ob'ects; ſtill there will remain an abſurdity, for it really had no pleaſing effect on the mind of Amelia, but the direct contrary. Something ſimple, like the following, verſified, would ſurely have been preferable. ‘ *To thee the thunder's voice need give no* ‘ *terror, and the lightning's ſhaft muſt* ‘ *paſs over thee harmleſs.*’

> ———From his cold embrace
> (Myſterious heav'n!) that moment to the
>   ground,
> A blacken'd corſe, was ſtruck the beauteous
>   maid.
> But who can paint the lover, as he ſtood
> Pierc'd by ſevere amazement, lofing life,
> Speechleſs, and fix'd in all the death of woe!
> So, faint reſemblance! on the marble tomb
> The well-diſſembled mourner ſtooping ſtands,
> For ever ſilent, and for ever ſad.

The powers of the pencil and the pen muſt be unequal to the taſk of deſcribing the appearance of a perſon in Celadon's don's fituation. Perhaps our Poet has done all that could be done on the occafion: '*Pierc'd by fevere amazement,*' is language bold almoft to turgidity: to fpeak of the lover's '*hating life,*' is fpeaking of an intellectual operation, incompatible with the fuddennefs of the circumftance. It feems indeed fufficient to have faid, that '*he flood fpeechlefs,*' and '*without motion,*' as in a kind of temporary death,

> Speechlefs, and fix'd in all the depth of woe!

The defcription does not appear to be much enforced by the fimile, but the fimile being in itfelf an agreeable image, one does not wifh to lofe it.

Our author's defcription of the funfetting is another remarkable inftance of his peculiar manner:

> Low walks the fun, and broadens by degrees,
> Juft o'er the verge of day. The fhifting clouds
> Affembled gay, a richly gorgeous train,
> In all their pomp attend his fetting throne.
>
> Au,

Air, earth, and ocean, *smile immense*. And now
As if his weary chariot fought the bowers
Of Amphitrite, and her tending nymphs,
(So Grecian fable fung) he dips his orb;
Now half immers'd, and now a golden curve
Gives one bright glance, then total difappears.

This paffage is truly poetical, but very incorrect. The painting is ftrong, but carelefs; it is a group of beautiful, but inconfiftent imagery. The ' *fun's walk-* ' *ing,*' is an act that infers the fuppofi- tion of an imaginary perfon; its ' *bread-* ' *ening,*' is an act that can relate only to the real vifible globe of fire: the men- tion of the ' *fetting throne,*' again indi- cates a profopopocia, and the ' *dipping*' of ' *the orb,*' again implies a reference to the natural object. This would have been a moft mafterly piece of compofi- tion, if the verb ' *walk*' had been ex- changed for fome other not incongru- ous to the verb ' *breaden;*' if the ' *fetting* ' *throne,*' the unmeaning phrafe, ' *juft* ' *o'er the verge of day,*' and the bombaf-

tick

tick ' *immenfe fmile of air, &c.*' had been all omitted ; the gradual defcent and en-largement of the fun, its immerfion within the horizon, reduction to a curve and total difappearance, (all fine natural and picturefque circumftances) been regularly connected ; and the roman-tick idea of ' *Phœbus's*' chariot feeking the bowers of Amphitrite, been kept intirely diftinct, and introduced laft as an illuftrative illufion.

The ingenious Mr. *Mofes Browne*,‡ in his Sunday Thoughts, has a fine de-

‡ This eminent Poet is now living, in a very advanced age. His Sunday Thoughts above-mentioned, and his Pifcatory Eclogues, have great merit, but are little noticed. With regard to the firft, the religious nature of the fubject, and its being written in blank verfe, are fufficient obftacles to its popularity ; and with regard to the latter, againft every thing that bears the name of *pastoral* or *eclogue*, there is an irrational and ridiculous prepoffeffion. It muft indeed excite the indignation of a fenfible man, to find the works of DYER, SHEN-STONE, AKENSIDE, that excellent Poem Leonidas, and fome other modern productions of great merit, fcarce ever fpoken of, while flimfy and even nonfenfical performances of the prefent day are applauded.

fcriptive

scriptive passage on the same subject of
sun-set :

> See where at length the *downward-leading* sun,
> His low broad orb of *setting splendors* rests
> On the green *pillow* of yon western steep,
> In *smiling* radiance, bidding half the world
> Farewell, on speed to visit nether skies,
> Carrying morn, noon, and night in ceaseless
> change ;
> Each new swift minute round the peopled ball.
> Look how the *rapid journeyer seems to bait*
> *His slackening steeds, and loos'd to evening sports,*
> Shoots down obliquely his diverging *beams,*
> That kindle on opposing hills the blaze
> Of glittering turrets, and illumin'd domes,
> A prospect all on fire : till sinking still
> More and more sinking ; while to sight quite lost,
> His rays play upward in the fleecy clouds,
> *That swiftly pencil'd dress* a mimic scene
> *To fancy's eye*; of groves and whiten'd alps,
> And tow'rs romantick, rear'd complete, or waste
> In ruin'd majesty ; with interspace
> Of golden ether or Elysian plain.
> Then vanish quite as soon, and shift by turns,
> To tinctures of a thousand thousand dyes. †

† GAY's Poem, called Rural Sports, has a description of the sun-setting in the sea, in which there are
some fine natural images.

Far

Thomson's paffage and this have fimilar beauties and fimilar defects. This has many noble images, and an uncommon melody of verfification, with much inaccuracy. The ' *Sun's broad orb refting* ' *on the green fleep,*' is a fine picture as a real object; his fmilingly bidding the world farewell, is equally fine as a perfonification; but thefe pictures, by vicinity of fituation, deftroy the effect of each other. There is great poetical grandeur in the thought of the fun carrying day with him around the globe. Thomfon's fun is funk and loft in the ocean, and we think no more of him. Browne's purfues his courfe, and our fancy follows him to Mexico or Peru, and acrofs the vaft pacifick to China and India, till he re-appears in our

> Far in the deep the fun his *glory* hides,
> A ftreak of gold the fea and fky divides;
> The purple clouds their amber *linings* fhow,
> And edg'd with flame rolls every wave below.

own

own horizon. The word ‘ *ball*,’‡ is always a bad substitution for orb or sphere. The mention of ‘ *rapid journeyer*,’ and ‘ *slackening steeds*,’ forces the idea Phœbus and his chariot on the mind ; and the mention of ‘ *diverging beams*,’ instantly effaces it. The mountains, turrets, and domes glowing with the sun’s radiance, are most forcibly described in that simple expression, ‘ *a prospect all on fire*.’ The romantick appearance of the

‡ A fine line in one of Pope’s best pieces is almost spoiled by the use of this colloquial puerile appellation ;

But if eternal justice rules the *ball*.

Dr. Young was very fond of this word *ball*. In his Poem on the Last Day, he has several couplets that rhyme upon it, particularly one very curious one.—The last trumpet, he says

Shall pour a dreadful note, the piercing call,
Shall *rattle* in the centre of the *ball*.

Addison was ridiculed for his translation of the *Integer Vitæ* of Horace, where he represents the hero of the Ode as standing unconcerned to hear the ‘ *mighty* ‘ *crack*,’ but Young’s language here is far worse, it conveys the idea of peas in a bladder.

evening

evening clouds, which like that of other inacceffible profpects, often induces the imagination to form fictitious regions of fuperlative beauty and happinefs, is exquifitely painted by the ' *whiten'd alps,*
' *the towers reared complete, or wafte,*'
and the

' *Golden ether and Elyfian plain.*'

The diction in fome parts of this beautiful paffage is vicious, particularly where the ' *clouds*' are faid ' *to drefs a mimick*
' *fcene in fancy's eye.*'

Nature is rich in a variety of minute, but ftriking circumftances, fome of which engage the attention of one obferver, and fome that of another. Thomfon and Browne have both defcribed the fun in the act of fetting. Browne has reprefented the picturefque effects of its radiance on the clouds of the weftern horizon, and Thomfon has remarked the gradual extinction of that radiance, till nothing remains but one uniform colourlefs, and at length dark atmofphere :

Confefs'!

Confess'd from yonder slow-extinguish'd clouds,
All ether softening, sober evening takes
Her wonted station in the middle air;
A thousand shadows at her beck, first this
She sends on earth; then that of deeper dye
Steals soft behind; and then a deeper still,
In circle following circle, gathers round,
To close the face of things.

This passage blends natural description and personification in a very intricate manner. Both would have been proper, and indeed beautiful, had they been kept asunder. The gradual vanishing or extinction of colour in the clouds, justly discriminates evening, considered as a point of time; but as such vanishing or extinction occasions darkness, it could not possibly render evening visible or perceptible, considered as a person.† The prosopopœia, however, is in itself just and noble; Evening stands a con-

† Had the Poet been describing morning, he would have had the advantage of combining reality and fiction; the withdrawing or removal of the clouds or shadows, might have revealed to view the fictitious person.

Z   spicuous

fpicuous figure in air; ' *Confefs'd*,' in this place, is but a puerile alternative for *known*, or *diftinguifhed*, and ' *All 'ether foftening*,' is a phrafe whofe meaning can be only guefled at.

Thomfon, in the above inftance, has given, as it were, a real exiftence to his imperfonated object, by the attribution of action, and her ' *calling the fhadows*.' He has on another occafion thus realized a perfonification, by fpecifying the effects it produced on human beings.

> He comes! he comes! in *every breeze* the power
> Of philofophick melancholy comes!
> His near approach the fudden ftarting tear
> The glowing cheek, the mild dejected air,
> The foftened feature, *and the beating heart,*
> *Pierc'd deep with many a virtuous pang decline.*

This fine picture is greatly injured by a few words. The power fhould have been faid to come, ' *upon the breeze*,' not on ' *every breeze*;' an expreffion which indicates a multiplicity of approaches; if he came on ' *every*' breeze, he he muſt have been always coming. The glowing cheek, dejected air, and softened feature, were all viſible; conſequently might *declare*, or denote his coming, but the ' *beating heart*' could not *be ſeen*, conſequently could not *declare* it.

The proſopopoeia is a figure leſs liable to abuſe than the metaphor, but it is very frequently abuſed. Our author, as the late Lord Kaims † has juſtly obſerved, employs it ſometimes with impropriety or affectation. The following is a ſtriking inſtance of the finical, or puerile. Little maſter *coolneſs* ' *loſt*' among his *bluſh* of *roſes*, ' *dropping his* ' *dews*,' and *muſing* on the *turf*, or *by the rill*, is a very curious figure:

Half in a *bluſh* of cluſtering roſes loſt
Dew-dropping coolneſs to the ſhade retires ;
There on the verdant turf or flowery bed,
By gelid founts or careleſs rills to muſe. ‡

† *Elements* of Criticiſm.

‡ Weak minds and young minds are pleaſed with this fantaſtical manner. The Author of theſe Eſſays, when a boy, thought the above paſſage of Thomſon a very fine one.

This

Thomfon's defcription of the Nile, difcovers a rich poetical imagination, but it is defective in correctnefs. We find in it that common fault of an incongruous mixture of natural imagery and imperfonation. The river is traced from its fource, till its arrival in Egypt, and its progrefs and increafe are illuftrated by a kind of metaphor, or indirect fimile, drawn from feveral ftages of human life, infancy, manhood, and age:

———————————With annual pomp,†
Rich *king of floods!* o'erflows the fwelling Nile
From his two fprings in Gojam's funny realm,
Pure-welling out, he through the lucid lake
Of fair Dambea rolls his infant *ftream.*
There by the Naiads nurs'd he *fports* away
His *playful youth,* amid the fragrant ifles,
That with unfading verdure fmile around. *

† This kind of poetry has no foul ; it is cold and artificial ; the product not of the heart, but of the head. Pope, in his Treatife on the Bathos, well compares it to a tortoife, a heavy lump, under a fine embroidered fhell.

* *Murdoch,* our Poet's Biographer, feems miftaken in his fuppofition that this paffage is borrowed from Pliny the Elder. Our Author is indifputably indebted for his Defcription of the Nile to *Kircher.*

Ambitious,

Ambitious, thence the manly river breaks ;
And gathering many a flood, and copious fed
With all the *melio'd treasures* of the sky,
Winds in *progressive* majesty along :
Through splendid kingdoms now devolves his
   maze ;
Now wanders wild o'er solitary tracts
Of life-deserted fand ; till glad to quit
The joyless defart, down the Nubian rocks,
From thund'ring steep to steep he pours his urn,
Till Egypt joys beneath the spreading wave.

Fine versification is a powerful recommendation. The critick's charity is too often induced by it to spare a multitude of poetical sins. Fine versification we indeed have here, but we have also a strange confusion of ideas. Nilus, as river-god, seems first indicated; he is the ' *king of floods, &c.*' Proteus like, he immediately turns to real element; he ' *o'erflows*,' and ' *wells out*,' and becomes a ' *stream*.' He as suddenly resumes his personal character, and ' *sports* ' *a playful youth*.' Nile, the current of water, then suddenly appears with pro-

Z 3   perties

perties attributable only to that current, as ' *winding through kingdoms*,' &c. Nilus, the deity, is then again as abruptly introduced, ' *pouring his urn*' from one thundering fteep to another. Our author has few examples of what is termed the *clinquant*, or *concetti*, but he has defcended to it in the circumftances of the ' *Naiads nurfing the river*,'‡ and of that river being ' *glad to quit the defart*.' Here is another fpecimen of his affected appellation, in ' *mellowed treafures of the* ' *fky*.' To mention that the Nile was increafed both by the defcent of rain, ' *treafures of the fky*,' and the influx of rivers ' *gathering many a flood*,' will appear unneceffary, when it is confidered that the former muft of courfe be

---

‡ What the author meant by *Naiads* here, is difficult to determine. If he meant *fifh*, a fchool-boy could fcarcely have been abfurd enough to talk of ' *fifh* ' *nurfing a river*;' if he meant Pagan deities, he has almoft as abfurdly introduced the mythology of Greece in Egypt. In his defcription of angling, he feems to apply the term *Naiads* to fifh.

conveyed

conveyed by the latter. To atone for these faults, there is in the last line a most noble instance of a natural object, affording with great propriety a fine personification: Egypt, the tract of land, is covered with a beautiful body of water; Egypt the poetical person, ' *rejoices be-* ' *neath the spreading wave.*'

This passage might be easily reduced nearer to the standard of classical simplicity, by dropping the impersonations, and retaining only the metaphorical epithets. Those criticks, however, with whom bombast and strength are synonymous, will doubtless think the poetical *features* of the passage much *weakened* by such an alteration as the following:

> From its two springs in Gojam's sunny realm,
> The infant stream first seeks the lucid lake
> Of fair Dambea; then in playful youth
> Sports through green isles and ever-blooming
> groves:

Ambitious,

Ambitious, thence the manly river breaks,
And in its courfe by many a flood increas'd,
Winds in progreffive majefty along
Through fplendid realms, and folitary tracts
Of life-deferted fand; down Nubian rocks
From thundering fteep to fteep impetuous pours;
And Egypt joys beneath the fpreading wave.

Thomfon's defcription of the South
American rivers muft not be omitted:

———————The branching Oronoque
Rolls a brown deluge, and the native drives
To dwell aloft, on life-fufficing trees
At once his dome, his robe, his food, and arms.
Swell'd by a thoufand ftreams, impetuous hurl'd
From all the roaring Andes, huge defcends
The mighty Orellana. *Scarce the mufe*
Dares ftretch her wing o'er this enormous mafs
Of rufhing water: *fcarce fhe dares attempt*
The fea-like Plata; to whofe dread expanfe,
Continuous depth, and wonderous length of
    courfe,
Our floods are rills. With unabated force
In filent dignity they fweep along,
And traverfe realms unknown, and blooming
    wilds,
And fruitful defarts, worlds of folitude,
Where the fun fmiles, and feafons teem in vain,
                                        Unfeen

Unseen and unenjoyed.† Forsaking these,
O'er peopled plains they fair diffusive flow,
And many a nation feed, and circle safe,
: r fair bosom many a happy isle ;
The seat of Kamskis Pan, yet undisturb'd
By Christian crimes and Europe's cruel sons.
Thus pouring on, they proudly seek the deep,
Whose vanquish'd tide recoiling from the shock,
Yields to this liquid weight of half the globe,
And ocean trembles for his green domain.

Poets not unfrequently aim at aggran-
dizing their subject, by avowing their
inability to describe it. This is a puerile and inadequate expedient. The
p   s of a writer can be no standard

---

† This is a beautiful romantic thought. Dyer has
one nearly similar :—

——————————In their rough bewilder'd vales
The blooming rose its fragrance breathes in vain,
And silver fountains fall, and nightingales
Attune their notes where none are left to hear.

This is from that noblest of didactick poems, the
Fleece, to which our celebrated biographical critick has
done such manifest injustice. It would be no difficult
task to vindicate it against his objections.

for

for the judgment of a reader. Thomfon has here, perhaps inadvertently, defcended to this feeble art of exaggeration. To fay that his ' *Mufe fcarce dared to ftretch* ' *her wing over one river,*' or to ' *at-* ' *tempt*' another, does not affift us in forming an idea of either. Very different is the cafe, when thefe rivers are placed in comparifon with ours, and we are told, that to the former the latter are no more than ' *rills.*'

The human mind delights to expatiate in unknown regions. It has fomewhere been obferved, that the accounts of travellers, even if ill written, are generally fought and perufed with avidity; when fuch accounts therefore are recommended by a dignified and mufical expreffion, it is no wonder that their charms are irrefiftible. That poetical power which can convey us " to Thebes, to " Athens, when it will, and where," has fo forcibly reprefented the progrefs of thefe enormous rivers of the weftern

conti-

continent, that our imagination necessarily attends it, and beholds their vast desarts, peopled plains, and happy islands. The true sublime is exemplified in the idea of their rushing with such impetuosity, as to ' *repel the tide*;' and the thought of ' *ocean trembling for his green* ' *domain*,' though amazingly bold, is one of that kind, in which the mind (prepared by what precedes for somewhat extraordinary) readily acquiesces. Thomson's paragraphs often close with lines peculiarly strong and sonorous, and we have a fine instance of it here.

And ocean trembles for his green domain.

Our poet's description of a Summer's Noon, is very natural, and has great energy of expression :

'Tis raging noon, and vertical, the sun
Darts on the head direct his forceful rays.
O'er heav'n and earth, far as the ranging eye
Can sweep, a *dazzling deluge* reigns, and all
From pole to pole † is undistinguish'd blaze.
In vain the sight dejected to the ground
Stoops for relief, thence hot ascending steams

† From pole to pole, strictly speaking, is improper ; the poet meant from one part of the horizon to the other.

And

And keen reflection pain.   Deep to the root
Of vegetation parch'd, the cleaving fields
And flippery lawn an arid hue difclofe,
Blaft fancy's blooms, and wither e'en the foul.

In faying that as 'far as the eye can
'range, there reigns a dazzling deluge,'
and that ' all from pole to pole is undif-
' tinguifh'd blaze,' it muft be allowed
there is unneceffary verbofity ; but perhaps in this inftance the redundancy,
as tending to enforce the impreffion of
the image on the mind, is at leaft par-
donable. Exceffive heat undoubtedly
enfeebles the body, and has been fuppofed to enervate the mind ; this was
probably the circumftance meant in this
energetick, and almoft bombaftick line,

Blaft fancy's blooms, and wither'ev'n the foul.

Confidered in connexion with the foregoing, the following is certainly an anticlimax, but it contains fine natural
images. The mowers pafs their noon

not

not only in eating and drinking, but often in sleep also :

> Echo no more returns the chearful sound
> Of sharpening scythe : the mower sinking, heaps
> O'er him the humid hay, with flowers perfum'd,
> And scarce a chirping grasshopper is heard
> Through the *dumb* mead.———

The context contains a bold prosopopoeia, and another thought, which, though indisputably fanciful, contributes to the general purpose of fully possessing the imagination with the subject :

> ——————————Distressful nature pants,
> The very streams look languid from afar ; †
> Or through the unshelter'd glade impatient seem
> To hurl into the covert of the grove.

The Poet describes the impressions of heat on his own person with great feeling :

† A master of composition may sometimes hazard such daring strokes, and succeed. Writers of inferior abilities attempting them, will only produce laughable absurdity.

All-conquering heat, O intermit thy wrath,
And on my throbbing temples, *potent thus*
Beam not so fierce! Inceffant ftill you *flow*,
And ftill another fervent flood fucceeds,
Pour'd on the head profufe.   In vain I figh
And reftlefs turn, and look around for night ;
Night is far off, and hotter hours approach.

Thomfon, who has here fo fully ex-
patiated on the hot weather of our own
climate, has faid lefs of that between
the tropicks.   His introduction to the
fubject raifes expectations, which his
defcription does not fully gratify.   The
porch, according to the vulgar adage, is
bigger than the houfe.

Now while I tafte the fweetnefs of the fhade,
While *nature lies around deep lull'd in noon* ;
Now come bold fancy fpread a daring flight,
And fing the wonders of the torrid zone ;
Climes unrelenting ! with whofe rage compar'd,
Yon blaze is feeble, and yon fkies are cool.

There is evidently in this a promife of
fomething fuperior to the following :

See

See how at once the *bright effulgent* sun,
Rising direct, swift-chases from the sky
The short-liv'd twilight, and with ardent blaze
Looks *gaily fierce* o'er all the dazzling air:
He mounts his throne;* but kind before him
  sheds,
Issuing from out the portals of the morn
The general breeze, to mitigate his fire,
And breathe refreshment o'er a fainting world.

Armstrong, in his excellent Didactick Poem,† has described tropical heat in a negative manner, by enumerating some of the circumstances that render it supportable:

What suits the climate best, what suits the men
Nature profuses most, and most the taste
Demands. The fountain edg'd with racey wine,
Or acid fruits, bedews their thirsty souls;
The breeze eternal breathing round their limbs,
Supports in close intolerable air:
While the cool palm, the plantain, *and the grove*

* Our author has here again confounded the mythological idea of Phœbus and his chariot with the actual sun.

† Art of Preserving Health.

That

That waves on gloomy Lebanon,† aſſwage
The torrid hill that beams upon their heads.

The fifth of the above lines, '*The breeze*
'*eternal, &c.*' is one of the ſweeteſt,
as the ſixth, '*Supports in cloſe,*' is one
of the ſtrongeſt, and moſt ſonorous in
our language.

John Philips, the celebrated imitator
of Milton's ſtyle, a poetical, but bom-
baſtick writer, has deſcribed equinoctial-
cal ardors in another manner, viz. by
their effects on the human frame.

Nor leſs the ſable borderer of Nile,
Nor who Trapobane manure, nor they
Whom ſunny Borneo bears, are ſtor'd with
    ſtreams
Egregious, rum and rice's ſpirit extract.
For here expos'd to perpendicular rays,

† This periphraſis has a bad effect. The mention of
'*the grove that waves on Lebanon,*' inſtead of *cedar*, the
name of the tree, makes one think at firſt ſight that the
Poet, inſtead of deſcribing the Eaſt or Weſt-Indies, was
deſcribing Mount Libanus, in Syria.

In

In vain they covet shades and Thrascia's gales,
Pining with equinoctial heat, unless
The cordial glass perpetual motion keep
Quick circuiting; nor dare they close their eyes
Void of a bulky charger near their lips,
With which in often-interrupted sleep,
Their frying blood compels to irrigate
Their dry furr'd tongues else minutely to death
Obnoxious, dismal death the effect of drought. †

But there are other circumstances peculiar to these torrid regions, and Thomson has abundantly succeeded in his pictures of them: among these, none is
more highly coloured than the following:

——————————————Breath'd hot
From all the boundless furnace of the sky,
And the wide glittering waste of burning sand,
A suffocating wind the pilgrim smites

† Poets are supposed to have a licence for exaggeration, but PHILIPS had no occasion for it here, if travellers can be believed, who assert, that in the isle of Ormus,
in the Persian gulph, the inhabitants were obliged to
pass the night with the greater part of their bodies in
cisterns of water.

With inftant death. Patient of thirft and toil
Son of the defart! ev'n the camel feels
Shot through his wither'd heart the fiery blaft :
Or from the black-red ether burfting broad,
Sallies the fudden whirlwind ; ftrait the fands
Commov'd around in gathering eddies play ;
Nearer and nearer ftill they darkening come,
Till with the general all-involving ftorm
Swept up, the whole continuous wilds arife,
And by their noon-day fount dejected thrown,
Or funk at night in fad difaftrous fleep,
Beneath defcending hills, the caravan
Is buried deep. In Cairo's crouded ftreets
The impatient merchant wond'ring waits in
    vain,
And Mecca faddens at the long delay.

This is poetry indeed! poetry fuperior
even to painting. The Poet tranfports
inftantaneoufly from the defart to Cairo,
and from Cairo to Mecca; but the
painter could not have fhewn all thofe
places on one canvas, without a flag-
rant abfurdity.

Poetical defcriptions of tempefts have
in general fuch uniformity, that the
reader,

reader, e're he begins to read, knows
what he shall meet with, and almost
thinks perusal unnecessary. Thomson's
Thunder Storm however is of other character, it sufficiently demonstrates the
uncommon accuracy of his observation.
No author, ancient or modern, (so far as
I know) has described the grand elec-
trical phenonema of the atmosphere,
with such dignity and precision. The
diction, as usual, is rather too diffuse.

'Tis listening fear and dumb amazement all:
When to the startled eye the sudden glance
Appears far south, eruptive through the cloud,
And following flower *in explosion cast*,
The thunder raises his tremendous voice.
At first heard solemn o'er the verge of heaven,
The tempest *growls*; but as it nearer comes,
And rolls its awful burden on the wind,
The lightnings flash a larger curve, and more
The noise astounds; till over head a sheet
Of livid flame discloses wide, then shuts
And opens wider, shuts and opens still
Expansive, wrapping ether in a blaze,
Follows the loosen'd aggravated roar

Enlarging,

Enlarging, deep'ning, mingling; peal on peal
Crush'd horrible, convulsing heaven and earth.

Storms arise from all quarters of the
horizon, but perhaps oftenest from the
fouth; the mention of that point is
therefore equally natural and picturefque; fpecification of pofition always
gives a kind of reality to a fuppofed
fcene. The ' *fudden glance of diftant*
' *lightning*,' fhould have been followed
by the thunder heard remote, not by
the ' *tremendous voice*,' and vaft explo-
fion; thefe are introduced too early in
the defcription. The tempeft rolling
its awful burden on the wind, is a juft
and noble idea. This part of the paffage might poffibly be compreffed to advantage:

'Tis lift'ning fear and dumb amazement all:
When to the ftartled eye the fudden glance,
Appears far fouth eruptive through the cloud;
And following flow the folemn thunder rolls.
Long, dark and threatening o'er the verge of
     heav'n
The tempeft fwells, but as it nearer comes,

                                        And

And spreads its awful burden on the wind,
The lightnings flash, &c.*

The ' *shuts and opens, shuts and opens*
'*still*,' is obviously an attempt at making the sound correspond with the sense,
which notwithstanding the verses are
rather prosaick, is not wholly unsuc-
cessful. The explosions of a thunder
cloud produce a diversity of sounds,
which no language can fully imitate;
the lines here employed in endeavouring at an imitation, have been thought
to be noise without meaning. They
may in part, but perhaps not wholly,
deserve that character.

Follows the loud'n'd aggravated roar,
Enlarging, deep'ning, now flow; peal on peal,
Crush'd horrible, convulsing heav'n and earth.

Thunder sometimes seems a kind of
violent laceration, as if some elastick
body were suddenly released from confinement; this species of noise was per-

* The candid reader will observe that thefe alterations are given only to explain my meaning, when I talk
of claffical and correct compofition.

haps

haps meant to be expreſſed by the epithet ' *loſened*.' Increaſed or augmented ſound, is not amiſs deſcribed by the
harſh term ' *aggravated* ;' but after this
it was certainly ſuperfluous to talk of
' *enlarging*.' A new idea is conveyed
by ' *deepening* ;' but nothing is added
to the ſenſe by the word ' *mingling*.'
Repetition is very well indicated by the
' *peal en peel* ;' but what was intended
by ' *cruſh'd horrible*,' cannot be eaſily
determined. It is no very extravagant
hyperbole, to ſay of a violent commo-
tion of the air, that it ' *convulſed hea-*
' *ven and earth*.'

> Down comes a *deluge* of ſonorous hail,
> Or prone deſcending rain—wide rent the clouds,
> Pour a whole *flood* ; and yet its flame un-
>   quench'd,
> The unconquerable lightning ſtruggles through,
> *Ragged* and fierce, or in red whirling balls,
> And *fires the mountains with redoubled rage*.

Here is obviouſly another attempt at
imitative expreſſion, and with regard to
ſound,

found, the paſſage is certainly unexceptionable, but it has in other reſpects
ſomething to cenſure. ' *Deluge*,' in the
firſt line, and ' *flood*,' in the third, are
ſynonymous; the former gives an idea
to which nothing is added by the latter.
Poets, when intent on their ſubject, often unconſciouſly adopt the language of
their predeceſſors, without conſidering
how far the adoption is conſiſtent with
propriety; Thomſon's line above quoted, ' *And fires the mountains, &c.*' was
probably taken from one of Pope, in
this manner, for it does not ſeem to
convey any preciſe natural image:

—————————As when angry Jove
Hurls down the forky lightning from above;
On Arimè when he the thunder throws,
And fires Typhæus with redoubled blows.

ILIAD, B. 2. 290.

But to proceed,

Black from the ſtroke above the ſmouldering
   pine,
Stands a ſad ſhatter'd trunk, and ſtretch'd below,

A a 4   A luckleſs

> A lifeless group the blasted cattle lie ;
> *There the soft sighs with that same harmless look*
> *They were alive, and ruminating still*
> *In fancy's eye, and there the frowning bull*
> *And ox half-rais'd.†* ——

This is a striking picture, but its grandeur is diminished by minuteness. The lines in italicks, however graphical, had better have been omitted.

> —————————Struck on the castled cliff
> The venerable town and fairy fane
> Resign their *aged pride.*——

We have here another well selected and sublime circumstance. Zucarelli, a celebrated modern artist, in his painting of Macbeth and the witches, has greatly

† Ariosto, in one of his similies, has introduced some of these images :

> As when the thunder o'er the ether clears,
> Slow-rising from the stroke the hind appears,
> Where stretch'd he lay, all senseless on the plain,
> Where fast beside him lay his oxen slain ;
> And sees the pine that once had rais'd in air
> Its stately branches, now of human care.—Hoole

heightened!

heightened the scene of horror, by representing lightning falling on a distant
castle.

> ——————The gloomy woods
> Start at the flash, and *from their deep recess*
> *Wide-flaming out their trembling inmates shake.*

The thought of the woods starting at
the flash, has great poetical boldness.
The context is almost unintelligible;
one scarcely knows what to make of the
' *wide-flaming out*,' and the ' *trembling*
' *inmates*.' Perhaps the author meant
that the lightning fires the woods, and
drives out the birds and beasts that inhabit them.

> Amid *Carnarvon's* mountain rages loud
> The repercussive roar: with mighty crash,
> Into the flashing deep, from the rude rocks
> Of *Penmanmaur* heap'd hideous to the sky,
> Tumble the smitten cliffs; and *Snowdon's* peak
> Dissolving, instant yields its wintry load:
> Far seen, the heights of heathy Cheviot blaze,
> And *Thule* bellows through her utmost isles.

This

This is a moſt noble paſſage. Poetry here enables the imagination to comprize in one point of view, what could not poſſibly be comprized by the ſenſes. We ſee the rocks falling from the Cambrian mountains; we ſee the heights of Cheviot in flames; and we hear the thunder echoing through the remoteſt iſles of the ocean.

Our author's deſcriptive powers are equally conſpicuous, in his picture of the ſetting in of a froſt. The paſſage is graphical even to the greateſt minuteneſs, and is not juſtly chargeable with a profuſion of verboſity.

                              ——At eve
Steam'd eager from the red horizon around,
With the fierce rage of winter deep ſuffus'd,
An icy gale oft ſhifting o'er the pool,
Breathes a blue film, and in its mid career
Arreſts the bickering ſtream.   The looſen'd ice
Let down the flood, and half diſſolv'd by day
Ruſtles no more, but to the ſidey bank
Faſt grown, or gathers round the pointed ſtone,
                              A chryſtal

A chryſtal pavement, *by the breath of heav'n*
Cemented firm ; till ſeiz'd from ſhore to ſhore
The whole impriſon'd river grates below.
Loud rings the frozen earth, and hard reflects
A *double* noiſe ; while, at his ev'ning watch
The village dog deters the nightly thief;
The heifer lows, the diſtant waterfall
Swells in the breeze ; and with the haſty tread
Of traveller, the hollow-ſounding plain,
Shakes from afar.————

The ingenious author of the Elements of Criticiſm, under his head of intricate and involved figures that can ſcarcely be analyſed or reduced to plain language,† has adduced a part of the above deſcription, in example.

---

† To detect and explain nonſenſe, is no very eaſy taſk, it is like diſentangling a parcel of entangled thread or ſilk.   Dr. Young ſays,

Thought diſentangles paſſing o'er the lip,

But it much oftener entangles paſſing from the pen. A rich harveſt of theſe intricate and involved figures might be gathered from his works, and the works of his imitators.   Yet he could condemn bombaſt in others.

————The

——————————The diftant waterfall
Swells in the breeze.————

This cenfure however is not ftrictly juft; the paffage has no confufion of figures, but merely a very bold ellipfis. The fenfe is too obvious to be miftaken; the reader naturally fupplies the word that is omitted. ' The *found* of the ' diftant waterfall fwells in, or rather ' *comes upon* the breeze.'

Thomfon moftly defcribed what he had really feen, but from the defcriptions of others, his imagination often formed very ftriking and beautiful pictures. Such are his accounts of the vegetable productions of the Weft-Indies, and of the fuppofed appearance of the internal parts of Abyffinia:

Bear me Pomona to thy citron groves,
To where the lemon and the piercing lime,
With the deep orange glowing through the green,
Their lighter glories blend. Lay me reclin'd
Beneath the fpreading tamarind that fhakes,
Fann'd by the breeze, its fever-cooling fruit.

Deep

Deep in the *night* the mossy locust sheds;
Quench my hot limbs, or lead me through the
   maze,
Embow'ring endless of the Indian fig;
Or thrown at gayer ease on some fair brow;
Let me behold, by *breezy murmurs* † cool'd,
Broad o'er my head the verdant cedar wave,
And high palmetos lift their graceful shade.
O stretch'd amid these orchards of the sun,
Give me to drain the cocoa's milky bowl,
And from the palm to draw its fresh'ning wine.

—But come my muse, the desart barrier burst
A wild expanse of bladeless sand and sky:
And swifter than the toiling caravan,
Shoot o'er the vale of Senar; ardent climb
The Nubian mountains, and the secret bounds
Of jealous Abyssinia boldly pierce.——

—Thou like the harmless bee may'st freely range
From mead to mead bright with exalted flowers,
From jasmine grove to grove may'st wander gay
Through palmy shades and aromatic woods,
That grace the plains, invest the purpled hills,
And up the more than Alpine mountains wave.
There on the breezy summit, spreading fair
For many a league; or on stupendous rocks,

† This is a specimen of what Lord Kaims called
Thomson's false coin; a *breeze* might *cool,* but *murmurs*
certainly could not.

That from the sun-redoubling valley left
Cool to the middle air their lawny tops;
Where palaces, and fanes, and villas, rise,
And gardens smile around, and cultur'd fields;
And fountains gush; a world within itself
Disdaining all assault.————

The impartial critick never experiences sincerer pleasure than when he meets with a passage sublime, pathetic, and beautiful, and withal so correct, that he can allow it praise without abatement. Such a passage we may safely pronounce the following: the sixth line, '*still fond-ly forming, &c.*' is one of the finest instances of alliterative melody in the language.

Unhappy he! who from the first of joys,
Society, cut off, is left alone
Amid this world of death. Day after day
Sad on the jutting eminence he sits,
And views the main that ever toils below,
Still fondly forming in the furthest verge,
Where the round ether mixes with the wave,
Ships dim-discover'd dropping from the clouds:

As

At evening to the setting sun he turns
A mournful eye, and down his dying heart
Sinks helpless; while the wonted roar is up,
And hiss continual through the tedious night.

Nearly of the same character is the description of a man perishing in the snow. This is of considerable length, and I have been liberal of quotations; it shall therefore suffice to quote the conclusion:

In vain for him the officious wife prepares
The fire fair-blazing and the vestment warm;
In vain his little children peeping out
Into the mingling storm demand their fire
With tears of artless innocence. Alas,
Nor wife nor children more shall he behold,
Nor friends, nor sacred home. On every nerve
The deadly winter seizes; shuts up sense,
And o'er his inmost vitals *creeping cold*,
Lays him along the snows a stiffen'd corse
Stretch'd out, and bleaching in the northern blast.

Distress from accidents of this kind, must be not unfrequent in a mountainous and thinly-inhabited country, like Scotland. Thomson's imagination seems
peculiarly

peculiarly impreſſed with it. Speaking of a perſon bewildered by an *Ignis Fatuus*, he ſays,

> ———————————He ſinks abrupt,
> Rider and horſe amid the miry gulph:
> While ſtill from day to day, his pining wife
> And plaintive children his return await,
> In wild conjecture left.———

Our Author's deſcription of ſcenes of horror, derives great force from this introduction of human beings actually ſuffering amidſt them. The ſtory of Celadon and Amelia, and the three laſt quotations, are remarkable inſtances. Theſe illuſtrations however, though probable, are general and fictitious; but he is ſometimes happy enough to bring real facts in example; when he is deſcribing the violence of the cold in the polar regions, he mentions the circumſtance of Sir Hugh Willoughby, whoſe ſhip was frozen in, while he and all his company periſhed:

—Such

—————Such was the Briton's fate,
As with first prow (what have not Britons dar'd)
He for the passage fought, attempted since
So much in vain, and seeming to be shut
By jealous nature with eternal bars.
In these fell regions, in Arzina caught,
And to the stony deep his idle ship
Immediate seal'd, he with his hapless crew,
Each full exerted at his several task,
Froze into statues, to the cordage glued
The sailor, and the pilot to the helm. †

When he is describing the diseases of
hot climates, he instances their fatality
in the case of Admiral Vernon's fleet at
Carthagena. This passage has been
mentioned by Dr. Warton with just
approbation.

—————————You gallant Vernon saw
The miserable scene; you pitying saw
To infant weakness sunk the warrior arm,
Saw the deep-racking pang, the ghastly form,
The lip pale-quivering, and the beamless eye

† There is perhaps a little poetical exaggeration here,
the action of frost could scarcely be so instantaneous.

No more with ardor bright; you heard the groans
Of agonizing ships,† from shore to shore,
Heard nightly plung'd amid the sullen waves
The frequent corse.———

Thomson, in the course of the preceding strictures, has been considered chiefly
in his principal character of a descrip-
tive poet; the delineatory part of his
work affording the best specimen of his
peculiar manner. His poem however
has other merit, for it abounds with
noble strokes of pathos, natural philoso-
phy, civil liberty, morality, and piety.

† A bold but poetical metonymy, or substitution of
the thing containing, for the thing contained, of ships
for sailors.

F I N I S.